BABY OF THE WOLF

PACK LOYALTY
BOOK FOUR

AMELIA SHAW

CHAPTER 1

AMY

The morning that stick turned blue two years ago, I didn't celebrate like other expectant mothers may have done in the same situation. I turned around and vomited into the toilet bowl, for the third time that morning.

I'd been sick for weeks but hadn't thought much of it, putting the sickness down to stress from work, or maybe a stomach bug. But when I'd added up the dates and realized I was three weeks late on my period, I'd known it was time for a test.

Pregnant. Becoming a mom was the last thing I'd expected at twenty-three and still single. I couldn't blame anyone but myself, though. And luckily, or unluckily for me depending on how you looked at it, I knew exactly who the father was. I'd fallen, or rather, jumped, into bed with a guy I'd met at a bar. So cliché, and yet that's exactly how it happened. Not my usual style, but I hadn't been able to resist him.

Noah.

I couldn't forget him even though I'd tried hard ever since to do so. More than two years on and I still dreamt about him almost every night. When I look at his child, the daughter he'd made with me that night, a replica of Noah's piercing blue gaze stares right back at me.

I shook myself out of my reverie as I walked up the two flights of stairs to my tiny apartment. It was small, but it was rent controlled, and a short walk to my parents' house which was essential, since my mom did most of the babysitting while I worked.

I put my key in the door and pushed it open. "Hello!"

"Hey Amy!" Mom called out as she walked toward me, holding my daughter in her arms. "How was your day?"

"Mama. Mama," Trixie said, leaning forward, reaching for me with her chubby hands.

I dropped my bags, the exhaustion of the day disappearing into thin air as I pulled my beautiful girl into my arms.

"Hello baby. Have you been a good girl for Grandma today?" I squeezed my daughter tight to me and kissed the golden curls on her head. "Thanks for looking after her, Mom."

"No problem," Mom said, reaching for her bag which sat on the small table by the front door. "I put some soup on the stove and did some washing. You should try to get an early night tonight. You've got circles under your eyes."

Gee, thanks.

I sighed. "Yeah. Trixie hasn't been sleeping well. She's teething again, I think."

Her cheeks would bloom bright red, and she'd cry with her hands stuck in her mouth for hours.

"I think you might be right. I saw her canines trying to pop through her gums on both sides," Mom said, opening the front door to leave. "They're notorious for being the worst of all the teeth for pain."

Damn. I knew it. Maybe we're in for another sleepless one tonight.

"Thanks, Mom. See you tomorrow." I kissed her on the cheek and closed the door behind her.

I sighed, resting against the door and thinking about all the things I still had to get done this evening, before I could enjoy the luxury of going to bed. A bone-deep tiredness washed over me. A single mom's life wasn't easy, and anyone who said so was utterly insane.

Trixie launched herself toward the ground, and I carefully set her on her feet. "Are you hungry, sweetheart? Let's see what sort of soup Grandma cooked for us."

Trixie took off in the direction of the kitchen, running at a rate reserved for kids much older than herself. She was fifteen months old, but had been walking for almost six months already.

"Oh.... pumpkin soup." I inhaled as I lifted the lid off the pot. "From scratch! Grandma is the best."

Trixie smiled up at me in seeming agreement.

I settled us into our nightly routine: dinner, clean up, bath, and then bed.

"Such a big, strong girl, aren't you?" I said while dressing Trixie for sleep, and not for the first time, noticing how muscled she was. Her arms were thick and her biceps defined.

"Mama," Trixie said, reaching for the diaper beside her and handing it to me.

"Thank you, baby."

I dressed her into her pajamas and zipped her into her toddler sleeping bag. "Bedtime, sweetheart."

I popped her down into her crib and handed her the only toy she liked to sleep with, a gray wolf that my dad had gotten her for Christmas last year. At the time I'd thought it was such a strange toy to give to a little girl, but Dad said that Trixie had picked it out of all the toys he'd offered her at the store.

In fact, she'd been so adamant, my dad hadn't been able to convince her to accept anything other than the wolf.

He'd been right to give it to her, though. She loved it. She wouldn't go anywhere without the grubby thing.

I stared down at her and watched as she nestled into the wolf, clenching it with her chubby little fist, then she closed her eyes.

I snuck out of her room and sighed as I closed the door behind me. She was an angel when it came to her routine. I was really blessed compared to other moms, from what I'd heard. But the likelihood of her sleeping through the night was low, especially if those teeth were trying to come through, so I figured I'd better get into bed myself soon.

I walked into the kitchen and put away the rest of the soup, then flicked on the TV to relax for an hour. I deserved a little bit of adult normalcy, surely?

I had only stopped working for the first three months of Trixie's life, and I had no intentions of doing so now. Trixie and I were going to survive and thrive, with a little help from my parents but not much else.

My daughter deserved the best of everything, and just because I was a young, single mom, didn't mean I couldn't provide for her. Quite the opposite. The love I had for my daughter drove me like nothing else ever had.

I was dozing off around episode two of some supernatural drama on TV when a strange, high pitched growling noise came from Trixie's bedroom.

I jumped to my feet. "What the hell?"

I bolted toward her room. Had some wild animal managed to get inside? No way! The window was closed. Or at least, I *thought* I'd closed it...

My heart pounded in my chest as I pushed her bedroom door open. I looked around, narrowing my eyes in the dim light.

A growl sounded again, and I glanced in the direction it had come from. Toward the crib. I crept over, icy fear trickling down my veins. *No, not my baby.*

I looked into the crib, half afraid I was about to find a wild raccoon in there with her, but there was nothing abnormal going on around my daughter. Nothing at all. Trixie was fast asleep, her wolfy clutched tightly at her side.

The growl came again, followed by a sharp bark. I stared in horror at my daughter as her little mouth opened to make the noises that had woken me. Again and again, she barked and growled, her face contorting in her sleep as though she were fighting some fierce beast.

Oh, God. What the hell is happening to her?

I slammed both hands over my mouth so that I didn't scream and wake her. Instead, I just stared in disbelief as she snarled and chomped her little teeth together like she was biting down hard on something. Then she relaxed, her face clearing of any animal-like signs, and once again she was my angel, fast sleep.

I stood at the side of her crib, waiting for another showing of this strange animal-like side of my daughter, but it didn't surface again.

Exhausted beyond belief, I staggered back to my own bed and crawled under the covers, tears of worry streaking down my cheeks.

I had no idea what had just happened, but it was another thing to add to the growing list of things I didn't know about my baby. And unfortunately, I knew why I didn't know.

It was because so many of her traits presumably came from her father, a man I barely knew and had no contact with. Mom had told me that I hadn't walked until I was thirteen months and was super-talkative at Trixie's age. Mom described my physique as being 'Michelin man'. Dough boy soft.

My daughter was super advanced physically, and yet she barely talked. She was strong and fit in a way that toddlers just shouldn't be, and now made animal barking noises in her sleep.

There was also the fact that I was certain her eyes changed color at times. Mostly, they were blue, an electric, bright blue that reminded me of Noah, but I'd seen them swirl to yellow, or even silver sometimes, in a way that didn't seem... natural. My mom and the doctor had told me I was crazy when I finally got up the courage to mention it, and I'd never been able to get a good photo of the shift. But it was there. Something... odd.

Was that little piece of weirdness connected to her father, too?

Who was Noah, really? And what did he have to do with all of these strange things in Trixie's development that I couldn't quite explain?

I closed my eyes and pictured him in my mind's eye. He was six foot three, with a body most underwear models would die for. He had a six pack so defined that I had been able to literally run my tongue around every muscle, through every groove. And I remember how much he'd liked it when I did that.

The base, animal attraction between us had been so intense, it was embarrassing to admit how quickly I'd said yes and gone home with him.

Our eyes had met across the dance floor, and heat had flooded my body so fast my legs had trembled from one single glance. His blue eyes had darkened so much that they'd appeared black by the time he stood in front of me.

A few words were spoken—to be honest, I can't even remember what we said to each other in those first seconds—and then a minute later he was kissing me, pressing me into the wall behind us and making it clear for the whole room that he wanted me. That I was *his* for the night.

I hadn't been much better, gripping his shirt and hauling him into my suddenly-aching body. I'd needed him that night, in a way I've never needed anyone before, or since.

He asked me to go back to his place with him, an hour's drive into the forest.

I'd been terrified, but excited at the same time. Despite normally having pretty good common sense, with that intense, throbbing need clawing at my belly, I'd had no choice. That feeling had over-ridden whatever smart voice in my head had been saying 'don't go'.

I went home with him, much to my shame afterward. But at the time? What a night it had been!

We'd arrived in a small town I'd never heard of and once getting past the massive wall and gates that seemed to be designed to keep everyone out, Noah had parked in front of a log cabin that he said was his. We made it up the front steps, but no further.

He took me against the wall outside the front door because neither of us had been able to go another step without giving in to the craving. We hadn't even made it inside before my first orgasm had crashed into me. But it had been the first of many. Noah had made love to me all night, showing a stamina and level of care that I'd never experienced ever in my life before then.

As the memories of that night crashed over me, I shivered in my cold lonely bed, and the tears began to fall in earnest this time. Noah had scared me, on a deep level. My need for him, and my inability to resist him, was one of the main reasons I'd stayed away ever since.

Not to mention the shame. First, because I'd had unprotected sex with a complete stranger, and then because I'd stayed away so long since then. And the longer I waited to tell him the truth about Trixie, the harder it became to reach out. Even if I could find him, after that night, how in God's name could I tell him he now had a two year old daughter?

I'd never looked for him after that morning. When I woke up around dawn I'd walked to the nearest road, called an Uber, and gotten back into the city without a backward glance. I'd never gone back to the club where he'd picked me up. Never tried to find that town where he lived.

Now, I didn't think I could put off the inevitable any longer. Something was wrong with my baby girl, and I knew, in a bone-deep way, that her biological father would have the answers.

I fell asleep and dreamt of Noah, making love to me all night long. When I awoke, I began making plans for our trip to find him, and hoped to God I'd be able to locate that town that wasn't on any map.

CHAPTER 2

NOAH

The sun was hot on the back of my neck, and the pick in my hands was getting heavier as the hours wore on. The shadows of the forest nearby beckoned but it would be a while before I could go for a run beneath the cooling foliage and take relief from this incessant heat.

We had work still to do, for our village.

I stood up straight and stretched out my back, then wiped the sweat out of my eyes.

I called out to the men around me, all still working but, like me, moving slower than they had a few hours ago. "It's looking great, guys. Let's keep going."

I dropped the pick and reached for another fence pillar and my shovel. We'd taken down the walls around our pack months ago, but it was slow going to rebuild normal-height fences and more housing to accommodate the pack. Now that land was available, everyone wanted more space. We'd been hemmed in for too long, and now, finally, the Thornwood pack was reveling in its freedom.

"Hey, you okay, Noah?" Ronan asked, walking up to me and tossing me a bottle of water.

I caught it and twisted open the cap, then chugged down the coldness in a few grateful swallows. I wiped my mouth and grinned at my Alpha. "Yeah. Though that was much needed. Thank you."

"I don't mean now. I mean…" Ronan made a strange noise, almost a groan, and crossed his arms over his chest. He looked annoyed and uncomfortable, not normal traits for the guy I'd known my whole life and the leader of our pack.

I dropped my shovel and narrowed my gaze at him. "What's up, Ronan? You need something? Or…"

"No. It's not me. It's Kara. She was wondering if you wanted to come to the pack dinner tomorrow night?"

The pack dinner? Between us and Kara's old pack? Why would I want to do that?

I frowned. "Ah, what?"

Ronan stared heavenward as though this was the last conversation in the world he wanted to happen. "She thinks you might want to meet some of the women from Allara's pack. She's got this idea of playing match maker, and although I think she's crazy, I promised her I'd ask you."

I laughed; I couldn't help it. "Thanks, mate, but I'm fine."

I found it kind of hilarious that a guy like Ronan was so easily influenced nowadays, by his mate. Obviously a fated mate changed you, because back in the day, Ronan wouldn't have done anything he didn't want to. Quite the opposite, actually. Our pack leader had quite the stubborn streak. Except, it seemed, when it came to Kara.

Ronan tilted his head to the side. "So, you're already seeing someone we don't know about? Because that's the only answer I can give my mate where she'll be satisfied. That, or you're gay. And I think she'd still want to set you up with someone if it's the latter."

I stared at the ground, to avoid looking into Ronan's eyes while I lied. "Tell Kara I'm seeing a human in town. I don't need fixing up. But thanks."

The untruth ate at my gut, and unfortunately, Ronan didn't leave.

I dragged my gaze up from the dirt to see my Alpha frowning at me. "What?"

He raised a brow. "What do you mean, *what*? I'll lie for you, no problem. Kara's need to make everyone in the pack happy is driving me half insane, but I was kind of glad when she wanted to help you. You're a good man, Noah, and a great pack member. She and I both want you to be happy."

I swallowed the lump in my throat. "Thanks, man, but I'm all good. How is Kara feeling with everything?"

"You mean with the baby due any second? She's sick, and grumpy, but you know..." Ronan shrugged. "I wouldn't have anyone but her. She's good for the pack. And for me."

I smiled. "She is. We're all really glad you found her."

There was suddenly too much emotion in the air.

Ronan and I both coughed and cleared our throats.

"Right. Well. I've gotta get back to this fence," I said.

"Yeah. Great."

Ronan left and the awkwardness in the air finally dissipated as I got back to work. Surprisingly, the Alpha's visit had buoyed my spirits. He and his mate cared about my happiness. There was little else a Beta wolf like me cared about. And yet, the lie I'd told to get them off my back sat like a lead weight in the gut.

I'm good. I'm seeing a human in town.

I felt bad, not because I'd lied, but because I wished what I'd said was the truth.

There was only one woman I wanted, and that was the human I'd had a one night stand with around two years ago.

It was pathetic to still be pining, and I would never admit it out loud, but she was the only woman I'd ever been with who had left me sated and happy on a level that was almost a miracle. The sex had been mind-blowingly amazing. And sleeping next to her afterward in my bed had been bliss. Against my nature, usually, to bring people back to my own home, but I'd curled my body around hers and my soul had been at peace in a way I'd never felt before, or since.

When I'd woken up to find her gone, I'd searched for her, first through the pack grounds, then in town. I'd gone back to the bar I'd picked her up at, every weekend, for six months. There had been no sight of her. Nothing.

Unfortunately, I'd had nothing to go on but a first name and a description. No phone number, no last name. It was like she just disappeared into the ether.

I hated that I'd lost her, and worse, I hated knowing that she'd deliberately run away from me, when I'd thought our experience the best night of my life. I'd tried to forget her, but there wasn't a woman in my bed, nor a bottle of scotch in my hand, that had made me forget the way her body had felt wrapped around mine.

Perfection.

I shook my head and got back to work. There was only one way to sleep at night nowadays, and that was to work myself into the ground during the day. I needed to be physically exhausted, and then I could rest, otherwise my mind raced and my wolf howled, all for a woman I'd spent scant hours with and would likely never see again.

My obsession with her made no sense, except for one unfortunate belief. My shifter believed he'd found his mate in the little human Amy, then I'd gone and lost her.

Whether it was true or not that we were fated mates, didn't seem to worry my wolf. He was convinced, and because of that, deep down, so was I.

~

THE NEXT DAY, I woke up with the same gnawing pain in my gut that I always did. *Loneliness.* The sensation was cold and heavy, and made me want to pull the covers over my head and pass out once again. But nature called, and the morning sun shone into my room. It was another hot day, with work to be done, and I needed to harden up. Amy was gone, and I had to figure out a way to keep living.

It was pretty obvious to me, and likely others too, that I was existing, and not much else.

I crawled out of bed, went to the toilet, then walked back to the bedroom to get dressed. Draven, my housemate, was already in the kitchen cooking up breakfast, judging by the smell of charred bacon on the grill.

"Bacon's burning!" I yelled out to him.

"Shit!"

I shook my head at the clatter of pots and pans in the kitchen. He was young and a bit naïve, but a good kid overall. Compared to some of the other guys I could be sharing a place with, I was lucky to have Draven.

I pulled on jeans and a t-shirt, and headed down the long hallway to the kitchen.

"You want a coffee?" I asked him, going straight to the coffee maker to turn it on.

"Nah, I'm fine, thanks," he said as he pulled out plates and began serving us breakfast: toast, scrambled eggs, and crispy bacon. My favorite.

"Thanks," I said, taking the plate he offered me.

I ate without real enjoyment, appreciating the food more as a way to stuff my body with fuel, then washed the dishes.

Draven grabbed his tool belt from the couch and walked over to the front window, pulling aside the curtains to look outside.

I grabbed my own bag and stuffed a few bottles of water inside, and bananas. It was going to be another scorcher. Better to be prepared.

"Hey, Noah," Draven called out from his vantage point at the window.

"Yeah?"

"Are you expecting company?"

I frowned at the kid, who stood peering out like a peeping tom. "No. What are you talking about?"

"There's a car out the front of our place, and I don't recognize the girl in the driver's seat. Thought maybe you were expecting someone."

My heart thumped in my chest and my mouth went dry. Settle down, I told myself. After all this time, it won't be her. But I couldn't help swallowing hard before asking in a pseudo-casual tone, "What does she look like?"

"She's still sitting in her car, so it's hard to tell, but I think she's got blonde hair. Hang on... she's getting out."

If the woman was blonde, there was a chance it was Amy.

I raced to the door and flung it open, unable to stand the suspense.

There she was. The woman of my dreams, in the flesh. She stepped out of the car, her lips turned down in a frown as she shut the door, then twisted around to stare up at the house. At me.

She looked older, more tired, but just as beautiful as I remembered, with long blonde hair and a pretty, heart-shaped face that I'd never forgotten.

I had to fight the urge to run down the stairs and grab her up into my arms.

My wolf, so often dormant nowadays, lifted its head and howled inside me. Adrenaline pumped in my veins, and I shuddered at the intensity of all the emotions that rushed through my system.

She smiled in recognition and raised a hand to wave at me, though I noticed the smile didn't reach her eyes. "Hi Noah."

I jogged down the steps and stood on the same level, staring at her. She wore blue jeans, a black tank, and a red checked shirt over the top.

"Hang on a second... is that *my* shirt?" It was way over-sized for her, and she'd rolled up the sleeves.

This time, her smile was more genuine and her brown eyes sparkled a little. "Yeah... I took it the morning I left because I was cold, and kinda kept it. Sorry."

I shook my head. "Don't be sorry. I... ah... Are you here to see me?"

I should be calm. I should be cool, but all I could do was stammer over the fact that she was here. She was *here*!

What if she wasn't here for me? What if...

She nodded, cutting off my racing thoughts. "Yeah. I came to chat. Hope that's okay?"

Okay? "Sure! About what?" The fences could wait.

"I don't know how to say this." She pressed her lips together, then dropped her head and stared at the ground.

"Whatever it is, you can tell me."

Draven walked down the steps behind me and said, "I've gotta get to work. See you later?"

"Yeah, sure." I waved him off.

As he walked away, Amy gave him half a smile before turning back to me. "Who's that?"

"My housemate. As one of the single guys in town, I get lugged with the younger kids on occasion. He's nice enough."

Her eyes went wide and round. "You're still single then?"

There was a hope in her tone that made me long to reassure her. I'd waited for her. Had she waited for me too?

My heart squeezed tight in my chest and my wolf paced, impatient to have the woman he felt was our mate back in my arms. "Yes. Very single. You?"

She nodded. "Same."

Thank the heavens for that!

"Do you want to come inside?" I asked, gesturing to the house.

She bit her lip and took a few steps backward, reaching for the car door handle. "Yes, please. But I've just gotta grab something, hang on."

"Sure."

She was back. And single, and quite possibly, here for me!

My stomach was tight and my muscles trembled with excitement.

Amy stuck half her body in the car, looking for whatever she wanted to bring inside. A bag maybe? What had she brought? Something to show me?

She whispered something I didn't quite catch, then she emerged once more, and I fell back a pace.

What the hell...

"Sweetheart, time to wake up," Amy whispered to the toddler in her arms, a little girl with curly blonde hair, clinging to a gray wolf toy.

"Mama..." the little girl said, moaning in annoyance, then she opened her eyes and looked up at me.

There were my very own eyes, strikingly blue, staring right back at me.

That was when the biggest piece of my life's puzzle fell into place. Amy had left, and she'd taken my child with her.

My daughter.

Holy shit.

CHAPTER 3
AMY

I trembled as I stood before Noah, clinging to my child. *Our child.* A daughter he hadn't known existed at all, but now he did. I could read the recognition in his shocked gaze as he stared down at Trixie without blinking.

What was he thinking? What was he going to do?

Trixie made an annoyed noise and I hoisted her to a more comfortable position on my hip.

"Can we please go inside?" I asked Noah.

He was still gaping, frozen in place, his eyes wide and staring.

He may have been in shock, but I needed to sit down and feed

Trixie, or she'd have a melt down and that was the last sort of first impression I wanted to make.

"Ah, yeah. Yeah. Of course." He blinked a few times and seemed to come to his senses. Sort of. "Can I help you? Do you... Does she... have a bag or anything?"

I pointed to the passenger side. "Actually, yeah. Could you grab the bag out of the front seat? That would be great."

He rushed around the car, pulled out my massive black baby bag, and slung it over his shoulder. "That it?"

I could have cried, right there and then. Why had I waited so long to contact him if he was going to be this good about the news? This thoughtful and helpful? God knew, I could have used the parenting help over the past year or two.

"Yeah." I nodded at him, clinging tighter to Trixie. "Um. Thanks."

Noah hurried up the steps in front of us and opened the door wide. He didn't say anything else, just stood there waiting for us to move past him and into the house.

My heart thumped so hard I doubted I would have been able to hear him properly even if he had spoken.

"Mama," Trixie spluttered.

Right. Move!

I raced up the stairs, past the wall he'd first taken me against, and tried to ignore the way my body shivered in response to the delicious and decadent memory.

"Okay, sweetheart, hold on just a moment," I said to Trixie as we reached the lounge room and she lurched to get down and walk around.

I set her on her feet and put my hand out for my baby bag. "Thanks for carrying that. She needs something to eat."

Noah handed me the bag and I sat down on the couch, rifling through the inside until I found the fridge bag with the yogurt snacks I'd brought with me.

"Here you go, sweetheart." I held out the opened pouch and she raced over to me, taking the yogurt and sucking it straight into her mouth.

Noah walked over to the other couch and sat down on the cushions. His movements were loose, as if his limbs were a bit shaky. He stared at me with what looked like a hundred burning questions in his gaze.

I swallowed hard. How did I even start this conversation?

Noah's gaze dropped to Trixie, then flicked back to me. "She's mine."

There wasn't any question in the words, but I felt the need to respond anyway. "Yeah, she is."

He jumped to his feet and walked toward the small kitchen. "Do you want a drink?"

"Coffee if you have it. I've been up and driving since six. She's an early riser."

He didn't respond but busied himself around the kitchen.

I got down on my knees and started pulling out some of Trixie's favorite toys so that she didn't break anything in the house, not that there was a lot to break. No photo frames, or vases, or even pillows on the couches. No decorative items at all. Nothing spoke of a feminine touch, or even... a home.

"There you go, sweetie," I said, handing Trixie a box with blocks that she loved.

She sat down on the floor to play with them.

Noah walked over to me with a mug. "Here."

I stood up and took the coffee. "Thanks."

The whole situation was so stilted, and my nervous tension rose. I stared at him with what was likely a hungry gaze, but I couldn't help it. God, he looked good. Older, more tired, like me, I guess. But my belly was tight and heat flushed up my cheeks from being this close to him.

He was still gorgeous, with his bright blue eyes and dark blond hair. But it was more than just simple good looks that had me shaking. My attraction to him hadn't diminished at all but luckily for me, it had settled to a simmer, rather than the flash burn it had been in the beginning.

"Why didn't you tell me?" he asked all of a sudden, and my stomach lurched.

That was it. That was the question I'd been dreading from him for almost two full years. Why didn't I hunt him down and tell him the moment I'd found out I was expecting his child?

"Well, ah..." I walked back to the couch, afraid my legs might give out on me. "I..."

Anything I said from now on wasn't going to be good enough, so where did I even begin?

Noah plonked himself back on the couch, and I noticed he had a beer in hand.

I raised an eyebrow. "Is that normal for you? To drink at breakfast time?"

Hopefully not, because then we would have another issue to talk about.

Was I throwing myself at the mercy of someone with a drinking problem?

He glanced down at the bottle, then back at me. "Hardly. But this conversation needs a drink."

I kind of agreed. So, without further ado, I took a deep breath, held tight to my mug, and plunged on. "I... should have told you. But I wasn't sure how to at the beginning. And to be honest, I wasn't sure what I was going to do to start with, either. So I just put it off, then it got too hard, and I wasn't sure I'd be able to find you, or if you'd moved on... or...."

"I brought you here, to my home. How would you not be able to find me?"

Heat flushed my cheeks. The heat of shame. "I'm so sorry. I... the truth is, I simply didn't know how to tell you. And then somehow, I convinced myself you wouldn't want to know."

"I wouldn't..." His voice trailed off as his lips tightened to a thin line.

"I'm sorry," I repeated, in a small voice.

The words seemed so inadequate, but it was all I had.

He nodded slowly. "So, what changed?"

"What do you mean?"

"Why are you suddenly here?" He narrowed his eyes at me. "Is she okay? Do you two need help? Money?"

I shook my head. "Oh no, no, we're fine. I work and earn enough for us both to live comfortably. I've managed pretty well, I think."

And I had. I was proud of how I'd gotten by on my own. With a little babysitting help from my mom, of course.

"Then why are you here?" he asked. "Not that I don't want you here—I do. I wish you'd come back straight away. But why now?"

I inhaled sharply. "I have some questions about, well, you. If that's okay?"

Noah's eyebrows lifted up. "Yeah, sure. Go for it."

How did you ask someone about their family line in a respectful way?

When I couldn't come up with the proper questions, I changed the subject. "Your town has changed quite a bit. Wasn't there a huge wall around the place last time I was here?"

Noah nodded, a smile tugging at his lips. "Yeah, until about six months ago. The new Alpha... I mean, ah, our new leader, decided it was time to open the town up a bit."

"Alpha?"

"That's what we call our leader, or whatever. He's in charge around here."

I pressed my lips together. Did he just say Alpha? Was this some sort of military base? Should I even be here?

I stood up. "I shouldn't have come here without notice. I'm so sorry. Would you like to come into town and meet somewhere else? I can give you my cell number, and our address."

"No!" He bolted to his feet. "Don't go. I don't want you to leave when you've only just got here."

"But this probably isn't the time to ask you personal questions about Trixie."

"Trixie?"

"Yeah." I gestured to the perfectly well-behaved little toddler sitting on the floor. Thank goodness this was a good day. Being a toddler, it was pot luck whether or not she would behave, or be a little more demanding. "Her full name is Beatrix, but I call her Trixie for short."

I reached down and grabbed my daughter up in my arms, feeling the need to hold on tight. I'd had Trixie completely to myself for her whole life so far, and while I knew Noah wasn't a threat, it was difficult to adjust my instinct to protect her.

Noah stared at her. "She has my eyes."

"Yes, she does."

Trixie reached out to him, her little hands opening and closing as she tried to grab at his t-shirt.

I gaped, amazed at the way she was acting. "She doesn't usually go to anyone she doesn't know."

Trixie grunted and tried to dive for him when I didn't act fast enough for her.

"Whoa, honey. Wait."

"I'll take her," Noah said, rushing to grab her up in his arms.

A strange zing ran through my body when Noah settled her on his chest, holding her against him as easily as if he'd done it from the beginning. They stared at each other with such a look of wonder, and growing love, that my heart all but broke for the time they'd lost.

My fault. I kept them separated from one another, and for what? Because I was scared? Because I was afraid of rejection? Not just for me, but for her.

"She likes you," I whispered.

Trixie reached for Noah's face, patting his cheek.

"What's wrong with her, Amy?" he whispered back, as if not wanting to startle our child. "She looks so healthy—she looks perfect, actually."

Tears came to my eyes at the wonder in his tone.

Then he added, "But you've come here for a reason. And I know it's because there must be something wrong."

I swallowed hard and forced myself to forge forward with the questions swirling in my brain. I'd gone through a lot harder tasks than this, in my life. Namely, her birth. That had almost killed me. Quite literally.

"Well, Trixie is a little unusual for my family. She doesn't talk much, but physically, she is advanced. Really strong, and muscled, and fast."

Noah grinned. "Sounds like my side. We don't talk much until we're about three, but our reflexes and strength come in early."

He hoisted her up on his chest and wrapped both arms around her, holding her tight. He looked slightly awkward, but Trixie nestled closer, as if she craved his embrace.

"There's something else," I said quietly, fear creeping into my heart. What would I do if he didn't know what I was talking about?

He turned his head to look at me. "Tell me."

"Last night, she was fast asleep and dreaming, and started making really strange sounds."

"What sort of sounds?"

"Well..." I ran my hands through my hair, tugging at the long tangles. I wasn't quite sure how to explain it. "Barking. Growling. Biting. Sounds a dog would make, if I'm honest. Scared the hell out of me."

Noah's eyes widened, but beyond that, he didn't respond. The silence stretched between us.

I continued when he didn't say anything. "I mean, she doesn't see any dogs. I don't have one, and my parents don't either. I don't know how she would have even seen one, except in books and the occasional movie. Certainly not enough to mimic one in her sleep."

Trixie sighed and put her head down on his chest. Then she closed her eyes.

I put my hand over my mouth. They made the most beautiful

picture together: Noah with all his height and strength and masculine power, and Trixie with her sweet face and golden curls, trusting the man who held her enough to fall asleep on him. "What should I do?" he asked.

I shrugged, feeling confused, but my smile was genuine. "You're done for now. So, I suggest you get comfy. On the couch maybe?"

He did as I suggested and crept over to the couch, sat down slowly, then lay back.

Trixie crawled up his chest and settled her head into the crook of his neck.

Noah was frozen, his eyes wide with shock. My expression probably mirrored his.

But as the minutes ticked on, Noah's beefy arms came up and cuddled Trixie to his chest.

A sense of calm and happiness settled over me as I watched them. In all the different first meetings I'd imagined, this moment surpassed even the best scenario I'd created.

"I know why she's barking, and whatnot," Noah whispered, stroking Trixie's little back.

"You do?" I asked, perching on the edge of the couch. "Thank God! Tell me."

Surely there was a reasonable explanation for all the strange things about Trixie that worried me.

He looked up to meet my gaze. His eyes were an electric blue, but a silver mist swirled within them that wasn't usually there. Damn it! I knew I hadn't been imagining when that happened in Trixie's eyes, too!

"I do," Noah said, "but you're gonna have to keep your mind open, because I've heard that humans don't take this news too well."

Hang on a minute. Did he just say, humans?

CHAPTER 4
NOAH

Amy's mouth dropping open and her eyes widening in nervous anticipation of my explanation was not exactly encouraging, but I knew what needed to be said. How she would respond to it? Well, I couldn't exactly control that.

"Um, did you just say... human?" Amy asked. "Does that mean you're, ah, saying you're not one?"

I nodded, stroking the back of the little girl I held in my arms. She was so light and soft, and yet I could feel the strength Amy was talking about. She definitely had my genes.

Pride swelled inside me.

"I may as well just get down to the truth of it all. Are you okay with that?" I asked.

I knew next to nothing about the woman in front of me.

Nothing except for the fact that our attraction burned brighter than a forest fire, and that my wolf believed she was our mate.

How true that was, was yet to be seen. But the proof of our child, half human, half shifter, lay curled in my arms.

Did she like straight talking? Or should I soften it some? I wasn't sure. I hadn't known her long enough to make that judgment call.

"Hit me with it. I'm ready." Amy curled her fingers into fists and lay them on her thighs. She was thinner than last time I saw her. Probably from the stress of having to work to support them both.

Something I decided to change as of this very minute.

"I'm a wolf shifter," I said. "Everyone in this town is. That's why we live out here in the forest, away from town. We need the space, and we're pretty private."

"You...." Amy shook her head and frowned at me. "Say that again?"

My throat was thick, and I stroked my baby's back to soothe both her and myself, given the sudden tension running through my body.

"My whole family are wolf shifters. It's not like the movies. We're not "werewolves", or creatures that have no control over ourselves. We choose when to shift into a wolf, and when not to. And when we are in wolf form, we can hear and see, and feel, just like we do when we're human. So you never have to be afraid of me, or anyone for that matter, if you see us in our wolf form."

Amy clenched her hands together tightly in her lap and began to rock a little bit. What was she thinking? Was she about to freak out completely?

"Holy shit," she whispered. "I don't want to believe you, but I knew there was something strange about this town. About you. Something... otherworldly."

I nodded, feeling the heat pour through my veins from just

looking at her. Damn, she was beautiful. Her skin, and those dark eyes, called to me like no other woman ever had.

But I pushed my desire down. We had a lot of shit to sort out before we got back to that.

Amy swallowed hard, her throat working. "So does that mean that Trixie, is a... you know... wolf. Person."

I grinned at her. "The term is shifter. And honestly, I don't know. It sounds like she's already displaying characteristics of our pack, but we don't often breed outside our own people, so I'd have to ask someone who knows. An elder maybe."

"Breed," Amy repeated, shaking her head. "That sounds so strange."

"Not to us." I kissed the top of Trixie's head, and she gave a little sigh. I squeezed her tighter, amazed at the amount of love I already felt for this little one. "I can't believe I have a daughter."

Amy stood up, wrapping her arms around herself. "I'm sorry I stayed away so long."

"Why did you?" I asked. "Really."

She squeezed herself tighter. "So many reasons. Firstly, because I was ashamed that we'd had a one-night stand and I was pregnant to a guy I didn't even know. That isn't something I usually do, you know."

His gaze softened. "I know. I would have seen you again, Amy. I would have asked you to move in here if I'd known. I would have looked after you, and her."

"How was I to know that?" Amy hissed back at me, throwing her arms in the air. "I didn't even know your last name. I still don't. All I knew was that we had this insane chemistry, and a hot night... and then nothing. I didn't have your cell number or anything. Hell, it's taken me three days to find this place! Even though I was here before. When I left, I certainly didn't memorize anything about the place!"

She was panting, her eyes flashing with anger.

Trixie whimpered on my chest.

"Shh..." I rubbed her back, and then stared at Amy. "Don't wake her up."

"Don't give me orders about my own daughter!"

After a moment, her gaze relaxed and she let out a sigh. She ran both hands through her hair, pushing it back off her face.

"Look," she began, putting both hands on her hips, "I made the wrong choice. It's clear now. But I promise you that I have taken very good care of her on my own. I've worked hard, saved money, kept a roof over both of our heads..."

It was obvious she'd done a good job, and all on her own, but she hadn't needed to suffer the way she had.

I sat up straighter, wishing I could hug Amy, but not wanting to let go of Trixie. "Amy, I'm not trying to give you a hard time. But I have... regretted that morning for the past two years."

Amy's eyes went wide. "Oh. What do you mean?"

She sounded hurt.

I rushed to correct whatever wrong idea she had. "I mean that I wish you'd never left. I wish I'd woken up and stopped you from creeping away. There was nothing to be ashamed of, or apologize for. Our connection is undeniable, and I hope you'll give me, and our town, a second chance to prove that to you."

I kissed Trixie's head again so that I had an excuse to look down and away from Amy's intense stare.

I'd missed her more than I wanted to admit and there was no way I was saying any more now. Not when the only reason she was back was because she needed answers about Trixie's genetics. If our daughter hadn't shown any signs of the wolf, would Amy be here? Probably not.

I had to be careful not to scare her away. Because if that happened again, I might never get either of them back in my life.

Amy sat down in the chair with a sigh. "I had no idea you felt that way."

I wanted to laugh but swallowed down the impulse. "Of course, you didn't. We barely know each other, just like you said. But I want you and Trixie to be here, and I'll do whatever you need to prove to you I'm worthy of being her father."

"You want me here?" Amy whispered.

Damn it, she didn't let things slip by her.

I nodded, then tried to back track. "Yeah. Of course, I do. It's the right thing to do, for Trixie. Don't you think?"

"Well, I hadn't thought about you and I together." Amy glanced away, her cheeks red with a heated blush.

I smirked, knowing she'd just lied to me, then pulled my mouth back into a neutral line. She was lying, but there was no reason to point that out to her. She didn't understand fated mates, but I did. I burned for her, and she would burn for me. I would make sure of it, this time round.

But if she needed time and closeness to be reacquainted with those feelings, then I was more than happy to oblige.

"Great. So, you and Trixie can move in here, and I'll get you set up with the Alpha's wife so you two can talk and get more knowledge about what's happening with Trixie."

"What? No! I can't move in here," Amy said, shaking her head. "I have a job, and an apartment. My parents are expecting me for dinner tonight."

The very idea of letting my daughter go again was like a knife to the heart. I couldn't do it.

What did I have to say to get Amy to stay?

I sighed heavily, my mind swirling with options. What would keep her here, even a little while longer? Long enough for me to convince her we were right together. "But what about her wolf characteristics? They may become more frequent, and more obvious. Do you really want her around humans when she's developing her strength?"

Amy's eyes went wide, and a touch of regret for my exaggeration flashed through me. I still felt justified in saying it though, if the words kept Amy with me.

"Do you really think..."

"I think, now that Trixie is manifesting some signs, it's a lot safer for both of you to be here, at least for a couple of weeks. We'll talk to the elders, and the neighboring pack, see if any of them knows anything that can help."

Amy nodded, but tears filled her eyes. Was it because she was overwhelmed, or did she feel helpless? I didn't want her to feel either.

I wanted to help, and I wanted to make her life just that little bit easier and less lonely.

"Go open the left drawer on the desk over there." I nodded toward my dad's old desk pressed up against the wall near the kitchen.

She didn't ask why, but she got up and walked over to it.

"Open the drawer and grab the white envelope."

She did as I asked and brought the envelope back to the couch.

"Take it, and go pay your rent, buy some stuff you need for Trixie, whatever you want. A crib maybe?" I had no idea what my daughter needed.

Amy opened the envelope and gasped. "I can't take this!"

"Of course you can! Think of it as two years of child support. I don't want you worried about your job, or bills, or anything like that. So, go back to town if you need to, but take the money. Pay your bills for the next month or so, and then come back and spend time with me, here. I promise you won't regret it. Please, Amy. I want to do this for you, and for Trixie."

It was a gamble, letting her leave at all. What if I never found her again?

Amy nodded. "I suppose I could tell work I need family leave. And she'd need a crib and diapers, and some things for your house."

I didn't correct her when she said my house. Soon, hopefully it would be *our* place, and she wouldn't need her apartment.

But I was patient; I'd wait for that day.

Amy inhaled loudly. "I think I can do that, but I'll need to make some calls. Does cell reception work out here? Because last time I tried, I had to walk halfway back to town to message an uber.”

I laughed. “Of course we do. Check your cell.”

She stood up. “Are you okay to hold her if I go call work, and my parents?”

Would I hold my own child so that my mate could tell the world she was spending time with me? A rumble of laughter started up in my chest. I swallowed it back down with difficulty. Did she really need to ask?

I cuddled my daughter closer, breathing in her scent. “Absolutely.”

Amy stared at us, then popped out the front and shut the door behind her.

I couldn’t help the huge grin that stretched across my lips. How was it possible that in one single morning, my whole world had turned around in such a momentous way?

I’d woken up this morning with a hole in my heart and a gut ache that never seemed to go away. But now Amy was back, and she’d brought with her the best surprise I’d ever had.

Now, I just had to work out a way to keep them both.

CHAPTER 5
AMY

My parents were much happier to hear that I was cancelling dinner with them than I'd expected. Once I told them the reason, of course.

In fact, they wholeheartedly agreed that I should stay with Trixie's father until we'd sorted everything out. I'd been a little shocked they agreed so rapidly, but then again, they'd always wanted me to contact Noah and tell him about Trixie.

Next was work, and they were actually pretty good considering I was giving them next to no notice, but I hadn't taken any time off in the past twelve months.

When I went back to the apartment, I just had to pay rent in advance and get Trixie a crib so that she could comfortably sleep here at Noah's with me. Although, I had a pack-and-play back at the apartment that I barely used, and I considered using that one instead of wasting money on a whole new one. It might do the trick for a short time. Then we'd be right to stay for the next fortnight. Or longer if we wanted to.

As long as I could deal with the fact that Noah thought he was some sort of wolf... werewolf... what had he called himself?

I shivered as I walked back inside the house where I'd known the most incredible passion imaginable. How was I going to keep my hands to myself with Noah always within arm's reach?

He hadn't moved from the couch, but he had twisted around to lift his legs up and was lying back a little more comfortably.

My baby girl was fast asleep on top of him and looked so trusting and peaceful, the image of them both, in turn, relaxed me.

"How'd you go?" he asked.

"Everything's all set," I said, though my heart was so full I could barely speak. "Work is sorted, and my parents are happy. All is... good."

I was on an unofficial, and definitely unplanned, vacation. With my baby's daddy.

"So, you'll stay?" he asked, his gaze finding mine. "Here? With me."

I nodded. "I need to go back to the apartment for some clothes and things. The porta cot, blankets, bottles. But yeah... we'll stay. At least until we've worked everything out and I can understand more about what's happening with Trixie."

Noah nodded but his eyes shuttered a little, and he didn't say anything else.

I wanted to know what he was thinking, but I was too afraid to ask. He was so honest, more so than I'd expected from a man I didn't know well and who had every reason not to trust me.

There was a knock on the front door, and a man called out, "Hey Noah, you home?"

"Can you answer that?" Noah whispered. "He won't stop calling out until we answer."

"Oh, sure." I ran for the front door, pulling it open to stop whatever pounding knock was coming next.

The man on the other side of the door was huge and vicious-looking.

I inhaled sharply, clinging to the wood to try and avoid automatically stepping back. Was he one of the wolf people, too? What was going to happen once he worked out I wasn't one of them?

Instead of growling at me, the big guy raised his eyebrows as if in shock, and then he hunched a little, making himself smaller. The deliberate act turned him instantly from someone scary, to someone who obviously had kindness in his heart. "I'm sorry... Is Noah in?"

"Ah, yes, but our daughter's asleep, so we're just trying to be quiet," I said. The term *our daughter* rolled off my tongue without thinking.

"Your... *what?*" The guy at the door spluttered, and I laughed a little at his shocked expression.

"Yeah, he was a little surprised too." I stepped back and gestured to the couch where Noah lay holding Trixie.

Noah lifted his hand and waved at the guy at the door.

"Oh, my God," the big guy said. "My mate's gonna love this."

Then he grinned and all the remaining fierceness in his face disappeared. "Hey. I'm Ronan. Alpha around these parts."

He stuck out his huge hand and I looked at it, before extending my own. "Nice to meet the... Alpha. I'm Amy."

He shook my hand briefly then dropped his arm away. "And you're human... I'm not sure what to say now. Did Noah tell you..."

I shoved my hands into my jeans pockets and rocked back on my heels. "You mean about the wolf man, person, thing? Noah just told me, but I haven't seen it in action yet."

And part of me still didn't believe him. Men turning into wolves? Seriously.

Ronan's gaze shot to Noah. "You know the rules."

His tone was accusatory.

"What rules?" I asked, feeling defensive of Noah. I'd gotten him in trouble already. *Shit.*

The Alpha turned to look at me. "We don't usually tell humans what we are."

I laughed, then put my hand over my mouth. "Sorry. That was inappropriate. But maybe you should. If I'd known, I might not have gotten pregnant, and then found my daughter growling and howling in the night."

I wasn't sure anything could have stopped me the night we conceived Trixie, but a little heads up might have done the trick.

"Sorry." The Alpha blinked a few times. "What?"

I gave the Alpha a quick run-down on the past two years, and by the time I was done, he'd invited himself in and sat down on the couch next to me.

"Wow. What a story," Ronan said, grinning. "I will see to Draven being reassigned straight away."

He got to his feet and headed toward the front door.

Shit. These people did not mess about.

I called out to him, quietly as not to disturb Trixie. "Oh, we don't want to inconvenience anyone."

"It's no trouble."

Trixie woke up then, loudly yawning and mewling like a little puppy.

I froze, watching her as she opened her eyes and took in her father for only the second time ever.

She didn't flinch even though I half expected her to. Instead, she simply smiled at him, then pushed herself back so she could sit up.

"Hey baby, did you have a good sleep?" I asked, rushing forward to pick her up.

She came straight into my arms, and then I took her back to meet Ronan. "Um, Alpha. This is Trixie."

I wasn't sure how my baby was going to respond to meeting another huge man, but she reached for his face.

The Alpha came forward and offered his cheek to her. She patted it gently, then moved back.

Ronan made a soft growling noise that sounded more like a happy purr than anything else.

"She's beautiful, Amy." He turned to Noah. "And there's no doubt she's yours. Look at those eyes."

"Of course, there's no doubt," I said, slightly miffed he'd even brought it up. "Don't worry about that."

Several people over the years had accused me of not knowing who the father was, and suggested that was why I hadn't chased him down for child support.

But Noah had been the only man I'd slept with that year. When I'd met him, it had been months since I'd been to bed with anyone, and then I didn't go near a guy afterwards. Maybe that was another reason my poor starved body ached every time I looked at Noah now.

Ronan glanced down, looking embarrassed. "I didn't mean... I just meant... those eyes."

"Yeah, I know."

The Alpha cleared his throat and shuffled to the door.

Noah finally stood up and rolled his shoulders as though stretching his back. "Did you need something, Ronan?"

"You didn't turn up for work, so I was a bit worried about you. I've seen you dig a trench with a broken arm, so I thought you might be bleeding to death in your shower or something."

I shuddered at the thought, but Noah laughed it off. "All good, but are you all right if I take the day off? I'm going to drive the girls back to town to pick up some clothes and baby stuff. Then they're coming to stay here."

Ronan grinned. "Sounds like a plan. Just let her know some of the pack rules, yeah?"

Noah nodded, and the Alpha left.

"You're driving us back?" I asked Noah, turning to look at him as he walked over to us.

Trixie put her arms out to him, and he picked her up out of my arms as though he'd done it a thousand times before.

Again, my heart broke a little for them both, thinking about all the times he should have held her when she was a baby.

Oh, the things I would do differently if I'd known he'd be this good a father.

"I'm definitely coming with you guys," he said, shaking me out of my guilt-ridden thoughts. "I'm not letting you two out of my sight."

I grinned at him. "I won't disappear again, I promise. In fact, we should exchange numbers and details, like now."

He chuckled and walked over to the desk to grab a set of keys. "Am I driving, or...?"

I shook my head. So, we weren't discussing the fact that he'd decided he was coming with us. We were just doing what he obviously needed to do, which in all fairness, I understood.

I'd run out on him once before. He probably wanted to make sure it didn't happen again. But things were different now. Everything was different. I would not run out on him again. He had a right to know his daughter, and she had the right to get to know her father and his kin.

"Well, Trixie has to sit in a baby seat, so we probably need to take my car."

He rolled his eyes. "Damn it. I have a lot to learn."

I walked over to the baby bag and grabbed out my keys. "You learn fast when you need to, trust me."

Noah shrugged. "Okay. Let's go. And grab the money."

I reached for the envelope of cash still sitting on the coffee table with shaking hands. I didn't want his money—I never had—but not working for a month was going to eat into my savings something fierce and we needed those in case of emergencies.

Even so...

"I really don't need it—"

"I want to help," he said firmly, cutting across my words. "So use it for whatever she needs. Rent. Food, clothes. Whatever."

I finally conceded that he was probably right and slipped the envelope into the baby bag that doubled as a handbag. "Thank you. I appreciate the gesture more than you can imagine."

Maybe I could start an account for Trixie and leave it to grow into a college fund. Then at least the money would go to her and not me.

Noah opened the front door, and with our daughter held safely in his arms, called out to me, "Let's go."

We drove back to my apartment, and I packed a huge suitcase of stuff for me and Trixie: toys, blankets, and the porta-cot.

Excitement built inside me at the chance to do something new and different. It really did feel, strangely, like we were going on vacation. Even if it was just to a log cabin in the woods an hour away.

Noah was the perfect gentleman. He played with Trixie while I packed up all our things, then carried everything down the two flights of stairs without a single complaint.

Next, we had to deal with the cash I had floating around in my bag, so he drove me to the bank and made me put the money in my account. I refused twenty times, but the wolf man had a will of steel and in the end, I did what he asked for the sake of time, and my daughter.

Who knew what would happen in the future and maybe one day we'd need the cash?

For today, we were going back to the 'pack', and on to an adventure I wasn't sure I was ready for.

CHAPTER 6
NOAH

By the time we got back from town, Draven had already packed up his room and moved on. Where he'd gone to, I wasn't sure, but I was going to miss his cooked breakfasts. Even if they were burnt most of the time.

"Do you want to set up in the second bedroom?" I asked, opening the door and showing Amy the room that had been Draven's.

It was now empty, save the bed and a chest of drawers.

"Oh, yes, please. It's lovely," Amy said, walking into the room and putting her bag down on the bed.

I glanced around. "I suppose it is."

The room was large, the bed was hand carved, and the nice ruby red drapes on the windows gave the room a little splash of color. "Room for the porta-cot too," she said.

I hated the fact she wasn't moving straight into my bedroom but decided against offering her that option. I didn't want to be turned down, not today. My nerves were already stretched thin as it was.

A silence fell between us and I wanted to grab her, hold her, and kiss her. All the things I wasn't allowed to do. All the things I craved.

I clenched my teeth tight and forced the desires away. I needed something constructive to do. Something physical, that would distract me from thoughts of touching Amy.

"I'll go grab the bags out of the car," I told her.

I didn't wait for a response, just turned and went outside to grab the suitcases and bags she'd wanted to bring with her. I hadn't realized a baby would need so much... stuff. But what did I know about kids?

I brought everything in and dropped it in her bedroom, as my little girl toddled around the room checking everything out. She tugged on the curtains and examined the walls like they held a mystery only she could see.

My body was burning with energy and normally this would be the perfect time to shift and go for a run. But I didn't want to do that, not today. Not when everything with Amy was so fragile, the trust so thin. I needed to stay close by.

And I needed her to understand a little more about shifters and our pack, before I gave in to my wolf side and maybe scared her half to death in the process.

"I'll walk up to the shops and get us some dinner, if you want?" I didn't think Amy would necessarily want to buy a meal at our only eatery. People would stare and I doubted she'd be comfortable there at this early stage.

"Oh, that would be great. I'll feed Trixie and get her ready for bed. Do you have a bath?"

"Just a shower. Which you're welcome to use." I pointed to the room opposite her bedroom, across the hall. "There's a full bathroom in there."

She smiled happily. "Showering her is a two-person job, so I think I'll just wash her down with baby wipes and be done with it. Thanks."

I opened my mouth to offer to help her with showering Trixie, then realized how stupid that would sound to her. We weren't a couple yet, and we weren't a family that could be free and easy and comfortable with each other like that. Not yet.

I turned away and marched toward the front door. "Back in about an hour."

I headed out into the cool night air.

"Fuck." I ran my hands through my hair and squeezed my skull.

What I wouldn't give to have Amy naked before me once more, but I wasn't seeing any signs that she wanted me the way she had the night we'd met in the bar. She didn't look at me the same way, and I wondered what having the baby had done to her. Did it change her hormone levels to a point where it might be permanent, and she might not want me anymore? Ever?

I hoped not but what did I know about any of that?

I walked up the main road and through town, making my way to the only eatery we had here. It was run by Bailey and his wife, and they made hot meals similar to a pub meal in town. They also did take out, which would suit me just fine tonight.

I walked into the shop.

"Hey Noah." Bailey's wife, Maeve, greeted me with a curious look while wiping down the counter top. "I heard you've got a woman staying with you. And a baby. Is that right?"

I shook my head as I wandered up to the counter. "Why am I not surprised that you already know my most private business, Maeve? You got her shoe size and everything as well?"

Maeve picked up her pad and pen that had been lying on the

counter and grinned at me. "Not yet, but I will soon enough. What can I get you?"

"Two house specials, extra chips, and.... should I get something for Trixie? She's... fifteen months old."

If my math was correct, that was about right.

"Do you know what she likes?" Maeve asked.

"Nope. Sorry."

"I'll put in some extra chicken and vegetables. Something plain. Little ones don't like seasonings or sauces much. Will be about twenty minutes, love." She ripped off the paper and set it alongside the other orders.

"Thanks, Maeve."

She went back into the kitchen, and I wandered outside to take a deep breath of fresh, country air. Going into town today for only an hour was enough to make me grateful for the fact that I didn't live there.

Kit bounced up to me, grinning. "Heard you've got yourself a human girl! What's she like?"

I couldn't help but smile at the Alpha's younger brother Kit. He was all happiness and sunshine in a world where most of the men were rough as a bag of nails. But Kit wasn't, and that was fine by me. He was a good guy, a loyal shifter. A man who'd die for his family and almost *had* done so when Jaime attacked our pack a few months ago.

I'd always liked Kit, even though he was an unusual kid. But that day had proven to me, and a lot of others too, that he really had more heart than sense.

"She's good," I told him. "Her name's Amy."

"Amy? That's cool. So, is she hanging around?"

I nodded. "Yeah, at least for a while. I asked her to stay."

Kit came to stand beside me, then whispered, "Is it true she had your baby and you didn't know? Now she's back and you gotta deal with like a... two-year-old?"

I laughed and shook my head as I swung around to stare at him.

This town. Word spread faster than a wolf after a hare. "My daughter's name is Beatrix. She's not quite one and a half."

"Wow," Kit said, shaking his head. "That's crazy."

"That I didn't know I had a kid? Absolutely." I'd never even considered it a possibility before.

"I wonder what Lacey's gonna say," Kit said in a pseudo-whisper.

I grimaced at the mention of my ex. "Well, not really her business anymore, is it?"

Lacey and I had been on and off again for years. She'd been a good distraction while I was looking for, and waiting for, my fated mate. I'd always harbored some hope that I had one out there somewhere, and I'd refused to settle for less than that.

Meeting Amy that night had proven to me that those feelings of perfection were possible, so anything I'd shared with Lacey over the past two years had been me searching for a little comfort in the darkness.

But Amy was back, and I wasn't letting her go. I just had to hope that Lacey didn't get too jealous, or act out, because she could be a nasty bitch when she wanted to be. She was a pretty powerful shifter, too.

I shook myself out of the negative train of thought. "She'll be fine."

Kit chuckled. "Good luck, mate."

He slapped me on the shoulder and headed off.

I groaned. He was right. I had better give Amy a bit of a heads up about Lacey, before she heard it from someone else.

"Dinner's ready, Noah," Maeve called and I went in to get our take out.

"Thanks, heaps."

"Enjoy."

I took the aluminum rectangular dishes and headed back to my place, my heart aching with anticipation, and my excitement thrumming.

I pushed open the door and called out, "I'm back."

The extra bedroom door opened, and my gorgeous little girl came barreling out wearing nothing but a diaper. She was all chubbiness and bulky strength.

She giggled, her little legs pumping as she ran.

"I'm gonna get you!" Amy called, running out of the room after Trixie wearing a thin summer dress and her hair still wet from the shower.

"Oh, hi," she said, scooping the baby up into her arms. "I decided to have a shower myself while she just played at my feet. I hope that's okay."

I nodded, my throat thick and my body instantly tight with tension and longing. Damn, she was gorgeous. Such clear, beautiful, soft skin. And her scent. It rose around me, mingling with the smell of my soap to become something altogether exotic and delicious. I swallowed hard.

"Yeah. Of course. You guys hungry?"

"She's always hungry," Amy joked, "But let me just dress her. I won't be long."

Amy disappeared back into the bedroom with Trixie and closed the door.

I went to the kitchen table and set down the food. We just needed some cutlery and we'd be right. I grabbed glasses and water, then set the table for three. How Trixie would eat, I had no idea, but she may as well have a place at the table too.

The baby came running to me and grabbed me around the legs.

"Oh, hello," I said, glancing down at her.

She stared straight up at me, those bright blue eyes unnerving to a degree. It was like looking in a strange mirror, but that didn't make sense either. The child was only one year old, and a girl too, and yet I could see so much of myself in her face.

She made a noise, as if she wanted something from me, but I couldn't figure out what.

"She wants you to pick her up," Amy said, walking up to the table and smiling at me.

"Oh, okay." I scooped her up in to my arms and held her tightly to me. "Maeve put some chicken and vegetables in here for you, little one. Would you like some?"

I unwrapped the packaging and Amy made agreeable noises. "Oh yeah, she'll love that. Perfect."

We sat down to eat and I got to enjoy my first ever family dinner, with the woman my wolf knew was our mate, and the child we'd created together. I'd missed so much, since that night I met Amy. Her pregnancy, Trixie's birth. The first year of my daughter's life. I wasn't going to miss out on any more firsts.

We finished dinner, then we walked together to the spare room so that Amy could put Trixie to bed.

She went down easily in the pack-and-play in Amy's room, simply cuddling her little toy wolf and going to sleep.

We crept out of the room together and grinned as though we'd shared in a great and successful adventure. Then we walked back into the living room and sat down on the couches, just like any other two parents who had just jointly put their child to bed.

But the sudden tension in the room belied how easy and natural everything else had been about the day.

Amy jumped into the silence. "So, what do you do at night?"

"Watch TV. Go to bed early. The pub maybe. A friend's house. Whatever, really."

Probably the same sort of things she'd done before she had Trixie.

Amy stifled a yawn, though the action didn't look very natural. "I'm pretty tired. Trixie gets up early, so maybe I should turn in, too."

She gave me a forced smile then stood up.

I got to my feet too, my heart pounding in my chest. I didn't want her sleeping alone, in my house, while I tried to get some sleep in my own bed.

"I haven't shown you the rest of the house," I managed.

She swallowed hard, her pupils dilating to huge black pools. Was that desire I could read in her gaze? Or was it something else, and I was just projecting what I wanted to see? "What else is there?"

"My bedroom," I said, feeling daring, and then held out my hand. "Wanna see it?"

She glanced down at my hand, then nodded, reaching forward to take mine. "I'd like that."

I tugged her out of the living room and down the hall.

It was time to find out if the fire of passion that had raged between us two years ago was still present, or if it had turned to ash.

CHAPTER 7
AMY

I couldn't believe I'd agreed to go into his bedroom with him, but here I was. My legs quivered as I walked down the hallway, past the bedroom where my daughter slept and on toward the back of the house.

The silence around us was deafening, and out of sheer nerves I asked, "Do you have your own bathroom? Or is the one we used the only one in the house?"

I didn't care either way, of course. One bathroom, two. Made no difference to me. But I felt like I had to make conversation, or I would burst into flames from nerves and excitement.

"Yep. Got my own," Noah said as he pushed open a large door and indicated into a dark room. "Come see."

He flicked on the light, and I stared around the room.

"It's lovely." The room was made up well but was once again devoid of any real personal touches in terms of decor. I stepped in to the room; it was almost as big as the whole living area. "It's huge."

"Yeah..." Noah said from behind me, his words rolling over me like a vibrating massage. "I spend a lot of time in here."

I could see that. There was a small couch on one side and a TV. Then there was his huge bed. A bed I'd been in before.

"You know, now that I think about it, I've actually been in this room before," I teased, walking forward. "Just not in the daylight."

The morning I'd run from him, the sun had barely been up, and I hadn't taken the time to look around and study my surroundings before I left.

"Hey, I want to ask you something. Why did you leave that morning?" His question caught me off guard.

I turned around and stared at him. "I told you. I was ashamed of my behavior. Embarrassed beyond belief, actually."

And I had been. I couldn't believe I'd gone home with a guy I didn't know, had sex with a stranger, and then gotten myself stuck in the middle of the forest.

I'd gotten up and taken my independence back quick smart.

He shook his head as he sauntered toward me. "I'm not sure I believe you on that. It was something else, wasn't it?"

My heart pounded in my chest like a bongo drum, a tingle of fear zinging along my spine even as my core melted in anticipation of being touched by him again.

"No." I swallowed hard, my throat constricting tight. "What else could it be, than what I've already told you?"

He chuckled. "Oh, I don't know. Me, perhaps? Did you wake up, look down at my face, and realize you'd made a horrible mistake?"

He ducked his head so I couldn't read his expression, but he reached for me at the same time, sliding his hands around my waist.

"Was that it?" he whispered as he tugged me closer.

Our hips met and I gasped at the intimate contact, his warm breath on my face.

"Was it me?" he asked again.

I couldn't do anything to stop the way I responded to his closeness. I placed my hands on his broad chest and groaned at the heat that radiated off him. "I thought there was a fault in my memory when I remembered your heat. But I was right... You're super-hot. Literally as well as..."

I broke off and my cheeks heated as he laughed and finished for me. "Figuratively?"

He chuckled again, and readjusted his height to stand tall and span his hands out to cup my hips. "You're pretty hot too. And I don't mean in temperature."

The embarrassed heat spread from my cheeks down my neck and I found myself reaching for deflection. "Is that a wolf thing? The heat? Because Trixie has always been the hottest, sweatiest baby."

He smiled gently, as if he could see through my thinly veiled deflect technique, and I shook my head.

"Sorry. Not sexy to talk about the baby, I know."

Bad move, Amy. Bad.

"Anything you say is sexy, Amy. But I want to take you to bed. Will you let me?"

I inhaled sharply, fear of rejection clutching at my heart. "My body isn't the same since I had the baby..."

I was saggy in places that had never sagged, and thinner in places that were once strong.

He bent his head and kissed me gently on the forehead. He looked deep into my eyes as he said, "You're beautiful. So much more beautiful than I remember. I want you, Amy. So much."

I closed my eyes to block out the look in his eyes. The look that told me he was speaking truth. It scared me, that truth. But I wanted more. So much more.

I opened my eyes again, enjoying the feeling of his lips on my skin, and the closeness of his body to mine. Still the uncertainty dragged at me. I pulled away and stared up at him, worry making me second guess myself. "I haven't been with anyone since I got pregnant, and I'm not sure…"

My next words were lost as Noah cupped my face and kissed me, hard and firm.

Well, that's one way to silence the anxiety, I thought, and then I forgot to think at all as desire took over.

I couldn't remember what I was going to say next, but it didn't seem relevant anymore. My mind melted into pleasure. I didn't want to think. It had been so long since I'd felt anything but pain, discomfort, and stress. I deserved to feel good for a moment, surely? I wanted to just luxuriate in his lips, in his presence. In the love I had always held for this man in my heart. The love for the man who'd given me my beautiful, cherished baby.

A groan escaped my throat as he moved closer, grabbing my ass and hauling me against his body. I ached so badly for him, and although the fear of how much I wanted this man had tormented me over the past two years, now that I was here, I wanted nothing more than to dive into bed with him again, to assuage the ache deep inside me that had never gone away. Not since that night we were together.

I tugged at his shirt, wanting to feel his skin against mine. *Needing* the skin-to-skin connection, like it was some kind of wonder drug.

He pulled back and stared down at me. His eyes swirled with color, and I bit my lip to stop from moaning aloud. Far from being scared, the exotic nature of his wild side enticed me in as much as the man himself. Even with everything I had learnt, the animal side of him didn't scare me. Not in this moment. Not as much as I knew it probably should.

"Do you want me?" he asked, his voice deep and sexy.

I nodded. I'd never been asked such a thing and found it as confronting as hell. But I understood that he wanted to be sure.

"Say it. Please." He groaned. "Tell me you want me between your legs, making you come over and over again."

This time I couldn't stop the moan that escaped my lips. "Yes. Please, yes. I want that, Noah. I want you."

That was all it took for him to lift me up and kiss me again. I wrapped my arms around his neck and my legs around his waist, and kissed him back with all the longing in my soul.

He walked me over to the bed then fell with me so that I landed on the mattress on my back, still wrapped around him. He pulled away just long enough for us to tear at each other's clothes.

I wiggled to help as he stripped my dress off my body in a few easy pulls, and my underwear fell away just as fast. Standing up, he yanked his t-shirt off over his head and dropped his jeans before kicking them away.

I got one look at his gorgeous body before he was on top of me again, hot and urgent. I lifted my legs, encouraging him to enter me straight away. I ached for him. It hurt inside, like an actual physical pain. I'd been empty for so long, and no one could fill that void, except Noah.

Instead of thrusting inside of me, he pulled back and began working his way down my body, kissing my throat, kneading my breasts, and generally tormenting me with this build-up of pleasure.

"No. Please." I tugged at him. He was going the wrong way.

He glanced up and frowned at me. "What's wrong?"

"I want you inside me." It was almost shocking to say the words, but if that was what I needed to say to get him to fuck me, then I'd gladly oblige.

He didn't come up to me like I wanted. He grinned like the wolf in the Little Red Riding Hood fable, and continued to devour me, inch by shocking inch.

"No... no...." I cried out as he kissed my belly then held open my thighs. "You shouldn't..."

"Oh, I most definitely should..." He growled, then flicked his tongue over my throbbing clit.

I exploded, jerking beneath his mouth and crying out as my first orgasm hit in a wave of pleasure.

He groaned and set his mouth over me, sucking at my clit while I grabbed for his head, anything to anchor me in the storm of passion.

He didn't stop his pleasuring. He licked me and suckled my tender flesh until I was peaking once more.

"Noah... please."

He thrust his fingers up inside me and my pussy clamped down on him, greedy and wanting more.

He worked me from the inside and the outside, and I was helpless to do anything but writhe on the bed and cry out to the gods above to slow the torment as wave after wave of pleasure washed over my starved system.

This is what I remembered from that night. The unending pleasure crashing over me in waves. I had missed this with Noah, so damn much...

I gasped and arched my back, my belly tightening to a crescendo once more under his talented fingers and tongue.

Finally, he withdrew and climbed back between my legs. "This time we come together."

He set his thick cock at my entrance and nudged at my flesh. I tilted my hips up to him, opening for him eagerly.

As if we were made for each other.

Yes. Please.

He slid inside me slowly, and I gasped at the slight pain as I stretched wide. "You're too big."

He shook his head and moved over me so we were touching from our noses, all the way down our bodies. "No. You're just tight. I'll be gentle, don't worry."

I didn't want gentle, but as he forged slowly inside me, I held my breath, waiting for more pain.

He was as gentle as he promised he would be. He rocked his hips slowly, thrusting into me deeper and deeper until he was finally buried to the hilt and the need clawing at me was at its peak. I was so tight, and hot, and sweaty, it felt like I would explode if he didn't move. Now.

I sunk my teeth into his shoulder, loving the salty taste of sweat on his skin. "More. Please."

He growled above me, the sound as dangerous as it was sexy.

I should have been afraid of the animal he'd told me was lurking inside of him. Instead, I lifted my thighs, wrapping them tight around his waist, and held on for the ride.

He pulled back then thrust into me, hard.

I gasped and clung to him tighter.

He did it again, and again, until he was fucking me into the mattress, into the headboard. I was crying out, he was growling, and all of it was a mess of pleasure and yearning and pure, unadulterated need.

I came on him once, then twice, rippling around his ever-hard cock, but he kept pounding into me.

The sweat rolled down his back, and the pleasure inside me kept building, until I reached up for his face and dragged him down to kiss me. Our lips met, and he thrust into me one more time before he came.

His tongue plundered my mouth as heat flooded my belly.

I threw my head back and screamed as orgasm after orgasm hit me, over and over again. The waves of sensation didn't stop until finally, he collapsed on top of me, and my mind let the world go, falling into the deepest sleep I'd had in years.

CHAPTER 8
NOAH

Waking up an hour later to find Amy still beneath me was a shock. I'd never passed out during sex before, but it had felt like she practically ripped my soul from my body in that last exchange.

She was breathing softly, fast asleep, and my sated cock lay on the sheets between us. I pushed up with my arms and moved off her slowly, not wanting to disturb her. Then I gently nudged at her shoulder until she rolled over and I could spoon her from behind.

She moaned a little, then nestled in and went back to sleep.

I glanced at the door, still wide open. We would hear the baby in the night if she needed us.

I smiled as I closed my eyes and put my head on the pillow beside hers. The baby... *our* baby. Despite how new the idea was, that was a concept I could get used to.

~

WHEN I WOKE up the next time, the sun was shining and the warm body in my bed was gone.

My heart plummeted and I jerked upright, for a moment reliving the last night of passion we'd shared. And its aftermath.

Shit. I called out, "Amy?"

She couldn't have gone far. Surely?

Please don't tell me you've run off on me again.

She didn't answer so I rolled out of bed and quickly pulled on my jeans before heading off to find her, my heart beating unnaturally fast. She wouldn't have left me again, would she? Not after all her promises?

The fear tugged at me, so I hurried down to the baby's room to make sure she was still there.

"Ah, there you are," I said, releasing a sigh at the sight of Amy in the spare bedroom, now known informally in my head as *Trixie's room.* She was lying on the bed next to our baby, who was drinking a bottle.

"Oh hey. I didn't mean to wake you," Amy said, sitting up on the mattress.

"You didn't." I walked over to where she was resting in an over-sized t-shirt. "Will she go back to sleep, or should we take her back to bed with us?"

"Oh, she won't sleep anymore," Amy said, swaying in place, her eyes half closed. "But I sure as hell could. After last night..."

She sent a slightly shy smile my way, and then shook herself and made to stand up.

I put out a hand to her, staying her movement.

"Why don't you go back to sleep?" I said. "I'll take Trixie out to see the town, assuming that's okay with you?"

Amy frowned. "Oh, I don't know. She's never been here before."

And Amy had never trusted me with her before. That part I understood.

"How about I just take her for a walk to the store, get some milk, and come back? Give you an extra hour? Is she fed and warm enough?"

Trixie handed her mother the bottle, rolled over, and crawled straight to me.

Amy rubbed her eyes. "She's okay in her pajamas. And her diaper's changed and her belly's full. She's okay for an hour or so. But... just don't put her down. She'll run off and she's really fast."

I almost laughed. Of course, Trixie was fast. She was a shifter's daughter. But then, with me being the shifter in question, I knew she'd be safe with me.

"I'm sure I can catch her, hon, but I have no problem carrying her. She's light," I said, picking up the little one and stepping toward the door. I flicked the switch to turn off the light. "You sleep there. We'll be back in an hour."

"Come straight back if she's any trouble," Amy said, though she was already pulling a blanket over her body. "A little more sleep would be amazing. Thank you."

I shut the door quietly and crept back to my room with Trixie to finish getting dressed and pull on some boots.

"What do you think, little one?" I asked my daughter as I popped her on the floor and went in search of a pair of a fresh t-shirt and a hoodie. "Wanna go meet your grandmother?"

My mom would freak when she found out I had a daughter I never knew about. It was probably better that I tell her first, if she didn't already know. This town was like most small towns. Gossip, especially the juicy kind, spread quickly.

While I pulled on some clothes and shoes, Trixie played happily with her little wolf toy

"Gray too," I said with a laugh. "Just like me."

Once dressed, shoes and all, I picked her up and crept out of the house. As soon as I'd shut the front door, I grinned at my little girl. "Your mommy is tired. What have you been doing to her for the past year and a bit?"

Trixie patted me on the face, then pointed to the road ahead.

"You want to go walking? Exploring? Yeah, I bet you do. Let's go."

I'd never had to talk to myself like this before, but it felt strangely normal to chatter away while Trixie listened.

It was early, even for wolves. Barely six a.m. I walked through the town, pointing at things as I went. The birds in the trees. The houses and the people. Even the shops that were still closed, except the small bakery. The staff there would have been baking bread since before four in the morning.

"Should we go in, sweetheart?" I asked her, and she reached for the door handle.

"I'll take that as a yes, and we'll get your mommy, and mine, some fresh bread."

I walked through the door and froze when I saw the woman behind the counter. *Hell.* "Lacey. I didn't realize you were working here."

Lacey was stocking the shelves when her dark gaze landed on me, then slid across to my daughter. Her eyebrows lifted in a way that would have been comical, if I weren't suddenly full of concern for Trixie and Amy. "Who's that?" she said.

"This is Trixie," I said, though my mouth was dry. "Can we get a couple loaves of white bread? Just put it on my tab."

We didn't carry a lot of cash around town, but I settled my tabs at the end of every month.

Lacey turned away with a flick of her dark ponytail and grabbed the bread I wanted from the shelf behind her.

When I stepped closer to pick up the bags, Lacey hissed in surprise.

"She has your eyes." Her gaze clashed with mine as she asked, "Why the fuck does she have your eyes?"

Trixie squirmed a little in my arms and then began to cry, clawing at me to snuggle closer. I hoisted her higher on my chest, her little hands grabbing at my neck and her face dropping into the crook of my neck, most likely to get away from Lacey's vitriolic gaze and tone. "Thanks for that," I muttered to Lacey.

I turned and walked out of the bakery, half afraid Lacey would follow me. Not that I was worried about her for my sake, but Trixie was still sobbing, and I didn't want her more upset.

"Come here, little one. It's okay." I pulled her around to the front of my chest and held her tighter against me. "She's just a mean girl that you don't have to see again. Don't worry."

Trixie settled down as we walked further away from the bakery. She could read a room, that was for sure, even at her age. A good skill to have.

"Let's go see if Grandma is awake."

My mom was going to be—I wasn't quite sure. Furious? Surprised? Elated? She didn't have any other grandchildren, since I didn't have any siblings, so perhaps this would be a good thing. I had no idea, and there was only one way to find out.

The strong scent of coffee brewing hit me as soon as I stepped up to the front door. "Hmmm." Then I knocked softly.

"Who is it?" my mom called out.

"It's me, Mom."

The door opened and my mom stood in the doorway wearing an old floral dressing gown. "Noah, what are you doing here so early?"

Trixie made a cute little gurgling sound and my mother's gaze darted straight to the little girl in my arms.

Mom's eyes went wide and her mouth dropped open a little. We both stood there awkwardly for a minute, until Mom blinked a couple of times and shook her head as if to clear her brain. She pushed open the screen door. "Who is this?" There was note of something in her tone I couldn't read. Was it... hope?

"Can we come in? I brought bread." I held up the loaves.

"Of course. Come in.Not just for the bread!" Mom ushered us inside. "Is she hungry?"

"She might be. She had a bottle a little while ago, but hasn't had breakfast yet." I followed Mom into the kitchen where she started immediately getting out plates and food.

She seemed to be bustling even more than she usually was. I wondered if maybe it was nerves about what she likely knew I was about to announce. Anyone looking at Trixie would know we were related.

She pulled out a piece of bread, cut off the crust, and handed the slice to Trixie.

"Here you go, baby girl," Mom cooed.

Trixie took the bread happily, gave my mom an enormous smile, and stuck the food straight in her mouth.

"What's her name?" Mom asked, still staring at Trixie like she was afraid she'd disappear.

"Her full name is Beatrix, but her mom calls her Trixie."

"Trixie..." Mom repeated. "She's glorious, Noah. But... where'd she come from?"

"Well." I shuffled my feet a little from side to side. "She's mine."

Mom laughed.

"Yeah, that's pretty obvious, Noah," she said, when she'd calmed down. "So why haven't I met this gorgeous baby girl until today?" She made herself a cup of coffee. "You want one?"

"No, I'm fine. And I only met her yesterday. I didn't know about her, before then."

Mom sat down with her coffee. "Start from the beginning. And explain everything."

I told Mom about the night I met Amy, and what had happened after she ran off.

"So, you think Amy is your fated mate? This... human?" Mom seemed surprised, and I didn't blame her. Fated mates weren't that common, and to have a human mate, in our pack anyway, was unheard of.

I nodded. "I do. I don't know how it's possible though. A human and a shifter. Fated mates. Do you know anything about it, Mom?"

She pressed her lips together. "I don't, but I heard from Kara that her sister-in-law is human."

"Really?" Kara and Ronan had met a few months ago and it had been obvious to everyone from the moment they'd set eyes on each other that they were meant to be.

"Yes, and she had a baby with Kara's brother, so obviously it's possible."

I bounced my baby on my knee, loving the way she giggled and laughed. "Obviously."

"So, what are you going to do?" Mom asked, buttering a piece of bread and cutting it into tiny squares for Trixie to eat.

"What do you mean?"

"I mean about Amy, and Trixie. Are you going to convince Trixie's mom to stay? Or are you going to let her go and visit every other weekend."

A growl rolled through my chest. "They'll stay."

I couldn't stand the idea of just seeing her for a couple of days every month. That would drive my wolf insane.

Trixie looked up at me, frowning. Then she patted my face as if to say, 'calm down'.

I forced myself to breathe slowly and evenly. They couldn't leave; I wouldn't handle it well. I wouldn't handle it, at all. "If Amy wants me to move to be with her, I'll do it."

"But you hate town," Mom reminded me, like I'd forgotten.

"I do, but I'll move if it means keeping my family together." There wouldn't be any other choice. I couldn't handle being so far away from Amy, or Trixie. Not again. The past two years had been hard enough missing Amy. But to miss my daughter as well... I couldn't live through that.

My mom gave me an assessing look, then nodded once. "You look well, Noah. Happier than I've seen you in a long time."

I looked down at Trixie, and unfamiliar emotions swelled within my chest. "I was missing something vital."

A knowing look passed across Mom's face, and her expression relaxed.

"Mama," Trixie said, patting my face again. "Mama."

"Okay, baby," I told her, getting to my feet. "I better take her back. Amy's probably missing her."

And I was pretty sure Trixie would be able to feel it when it was time to go back. She was an intuitive little thing.

Mom stood up and started packing food into containers. "I'll send you with some sandwiches. Give me two minutes."

I set Trixie down to run around, and when our picnic was ready, we headed home.

This was what I'd craved for more years than I cared to admit. I'd enjoyed playing around with women when I was young, but it had gotten old, fast. I wanted a family, a woman, and a real home.

What I hadn't known for the past two years, was that I already had a family. A woman, a child. They'd just forgotten to pass along the message.

Well now she was back, and I wouldn't let Amy go, not without a fight. I'd lost her once, and I wouldn't lose her again.

AMY

I woke up to the sound of a door closing, then Noah's voice calling out, "Amy? Are you up?"

"I'm awake!" I said, though my body was still heavy with sleep.

I glanced at the time on my phone. Eight a.m.? Shit!

I sat bolt upright in bed and swayed, "Whoa, too fast."

I swung my legs off the bed then waited for a minute. God, I was more tired than I thought, and my body definitely wanted more rest.

"Everything okay?" I called out. "Trixie behave herself?"

"Yeah. All good."

I got dressed slowly, my body aching with tiredness still.

"Come on," I told myself, shaking my head from side to side. A coffee, that was what I needed. Then I'd be all right.

I walked out of the room. Noah was unpacking food onto the table, and the smell of coffee permeated the air.

"Hmm, smells good. Whatcha got there, baby girl?"

Trixie held up her hands, both stuffed with what looked like white bread.

I glanced up at Noah, heat flooding my cheeks when he stared back at me with the same hunger on his face that he'd shown last night. He obviously hadn't gotten enough of me yet, which was reassuring and terrifying in equal measure. I was a little afraid to get too invested again, in my feelings for Noah. Next time I wouldn't have a little Trixie to assuage the heartache and the sense of loss when it was time to head back to the city.

With heat unfurling in my belly, I knew I hadn't gotten enough of Noah. Would I ever have enough of this sexy, enigmatic man? "Did you go to the bakery?"

"Yeah, it was the only shop open at this time of the morning."

He went over to the cabinets to pull out mugs for coffee.

I picked up my girl and sat down with her in my lap, hugging her sweet little body to mine. "Thank you so much for the sleep in. It was really great to have someone to help with her this morning."

That was something I'd missed out on, raising her on my own. Mom and Dad had helped when they could, but they'd left me alone to raise her mostly and that meant I did all nights, weekends, and mornings. It was a lot.

He smiled at me like it was nothing, but to me the couple of hours extra sleep, knowing Trixie was in safe hands, had been everything.

"No problem," he said. "We had fun, didn't we, little one? Oh, by the way, I took her around to meet my mom."

I picked up the mug of coffee and froze when it was halfway to my lips as his words registered. "You... what?"

"Took her around to meet her grandma. My dad died a few years ago, but at least my mom got to meet her."

Noah sat down across from me and I just stared at him. He'd... what? I couldn't quite process the idea.

"What's wrong?" he asked. "You look upset."

"Oh, no. I'm not upset." *Shocked. Worried, maybe.* "I just, uh, suppose I hadn't really thought about her having grandparents on your side of the family."

Noah snorted. "Yeah, I don't think you really thought about anyone in that regard, me included."

Horror slapped me right in the face. He hadn't sounded bitter, but what he'd said was correct. In keeping Trixie from him—and from his family—I had been very much in the wrong. "I know. And I'm sorry. Truly, I..."

I was going to have to apologize for my choice to withhold Trixie from him for a long time. Every time he mentioned it, I felt the need to run and hide from the shame of my actions and decisions.

"Don't worry," he said. "I'm just teasing you. We've just gotta make up for lost time."

He grabbed plates and served the food, which turned out to be cheese, ham, and fresh buttery bread.

"What did your mom say?" I asked, desperate to know if some older she-wolf was about to hunt me down for hurting her son.

He shrugged. "She was a little shocked, but she takes most things in her stride. She and Trixie seemed to take to one another, which was great to see."

"So, will she be coming over here to yell at me later?" I asked, only half-joking. "Should I be running for the hills again?"

Noah shook his head. "Don't worry about my mom. She's pretty cool, actually. And no, you won't be taking Trixie away from me again."

Despite his words earlier, about not to worry, there was an edge to his voice now. I swallowed hard at the thinly veiled threat.

I pushed back the need to fight him, because I was in the wrong and we both knew it.

"I won't," I said. "No matter what we decide about where we're living, or any of that stuff in the future, I promise you can always have access to her."

He made a strange growly noise and drank his coffee.

My heart ached. "Did I say something wrong?"

Again? He seemed different this morning. I felt a little bit as though I were walking on eggshells around him.

He shook his head and kept his gaze low, obviously not wanting to talk at the moment about whatever was bothering him.

I drank my coffee and ate some of the food, trying my best to enjoy our first breakfast together, but worrying too much over what he was thinking to really get into it.

Trixie grew grouchy and tired, so I put her to bed and cleaned up the kitchen.

Noah hung around, not really saying much.

"If you need to go to work," I said, "it's fine. I'll just potter around here. Clean up, make dinner if you show me where everything is."

Noah shook his head. "I'll stay with you today."

"Worried I'll run away again?" I joked.

His face went deadly serious, and his eyes grew dark.

"You are, aren't you?" I forced myself to ask, though my throat was thick with sudden emotion.

I put down the dish cloth and walked across the room toward him. "Noah, I don't know what else to say or do to show you how sorry I am that I left two years ago. That I didn't tell you about Trixie."

He crossed his arms over his chest and still didn't speak.

I pressed my hands together in front of my body. "I am so sorry, Noah. I really am. I wish I could go back and change it all, but I can't. I'm here now, wanting to find a way to make this work."

"Make what work, Amy?" he asked. "You only came back because Trixie is going to turn into a wolf shifter and you need some help understanding that and managing her. If it hadn't been for that, you would never have sought me out, and I would never have met my child. Never known I *had* a child at all."

He was huffing a little now, and I wrapped my arms around my chest to try and comfort that part of me that was breaking. I'd thought he was okay with it, in some small way. That coming back now had made up just a little, for what I'd done. But I could see now that it wasn't nearly enough. I wasn't sure if it would ever be enough.

"Noah..."

"No," he said, his voice harsh. "It's true, and you can't change that fact. I just have to get used to the idea that you didn't come back for *me*."

"What are you talking about?"

"Nothing." He shook his head, then stormed for the front door. "You're right. I probably should get some work done."

"I won't leave," I said, even though part of me was aching to run from all the paranormal craziness surrounding me. "I promise."

"I know you won't, because you know I'll find you two again."

I shivered from the rage in his voice, but shook my head. "That's not why. I won't leave this time, or any time in future, because you're already a great father, and I want that for Trixie. She should have had you from the start and I did her as well as you a disservice by what I did. I'm sorry she didn't have you from the beginning, Noah."

Noah growled a little then shook his head like he was deciding against talking further. He walked out the front door, slamming it behind him.

I stared after him, tears filling my eyes. What the hell had that been about? I sat down on the couch and let go of the sobs that had been building in my chest since this little fight had begun.

It had come out of nowhere, but it was clear that Noah was very distressed. Now, I was, too.

I grabbed the tissues nearby and balled some up, sobbing into them through the pain. I knew I'd done the wrong thing when I made the choice not to involve Noah in my pregnancy or the birth, and that mistake had haunted me ever since.

Now I was realizing that I would never again be able to make decisions for her and me, without Noah's involvement.

Was that something I wanted, that I'd miss? I didn't know. But it was a scary thought to have after being independent for so long. To be held accountable and liable by another human being… Well, was he even classified as a human? I had so much to learn about this life of wolf shifters.

There was a knock at the door, and I tried to swallow the tears. Shit, I needed to get myself together. I grabbed more tissues and wiped at my eyes.

The knocking sounded again then a female voice called out, "Hello? Is anyone home?"

I stood up and took a few quick breaths before walking to the door to open it.

"Um, hello," I said, biting my lip as the tears rose again.

I was such a mess. How embarrassing.

The woman on the other side of the door looked about the same age as me and had a kind face. "Hi, you must be Amy. I'm Kara, Ronan's wife."

The Alpha's wife.

I nodded but couldn't really speak. I should be able to pull myself together, but I was struggling today.

"Can I come in?" she asked.

I nodded and stepped back. *Get yourself together.* I wiped at the tears on my face and hoped to hell Kara was as nice as Ronan.

"I heard you brought a baby with you. Is she awake?" Kara asked, shutting the door then walking into the living room.

"No. She went down for her nap about an hour ago, but she'll be up soon."

I noticed the swelling of Kara's belly and the way her loose t-shirt clung to her. I swallowed the pregnancy question, because that was not a question any sane person asked another woman. I looked six months pregnant for at least a month after I had Trixie.

"Do you have any kids?" I asked her, settling onto the well-worn couch.

"Oh, I'm expecting my first in about three months," she said with a grin, cupping her hands around her belly.

I was happy for her. "You look beautiful."

"How was your pregnancy?" she asked, then groaned. "I've been feeling so sick."

"Oh, the pregnancy was okay. The birth, not so much for me. But that might have been because I'm human and Noah's, well... not."

Kara sat down on the couch opposite me. "So, you know what we are?"

I nodded. "Technically, yes. I've heard the words, but I'm not sure I totally... get it yet."

Or fully believe him.

Kara grinned at me. "Noah will show you his wolf when you're ready. I'd show you now if I could, but the pregnancy makes it almost impossible for me to shift, and then shift back. It's a horrible feeling, like denying half of myself an existence."

I shook my head. "It's such an incredible concept. I don't think I've grasped all of this yet."

Kara sighed. "Yeah, I can only imagine. I was born and bred out here, in a pack about an hour away. My brother mated with a human from town, so she's probably a good person you could talk to you about everything. I could ask her, if you like?"

"Really?" I asked. "There's more of us here?"

"Absolutely. And honestly, I think you'll love Tammy. She's so strong and fiery."

"I'd love to meet her," I said, because any type of alliance in this strange new world would be a good thing.

"Great. I'll set it up," Kara said. "But while I'm here, is there anything I can do for you?"

I shook my head. "Not at the moment, though I appreciate the thought."

"You wanna tell me why you're crying then?"

I sighed. "It's just... everything. I'm a bit overwhelmed, and Noah is angry about me keeping Trixie a secret for so long."

Kara sighed. "Yeah, wolf shifters have huge hearts and are the most loyal men there are, but they're also stubborn and have egos the size of a house."

I laughed at how aptly she'd put it. "Thanks for the tip."

Kara stood up and held out her hand. "Welcome to the pack. If you need me, I'm about three minutes away."

"Thank you, Kara."

She left, but my heart felt stronger. If I had some help easing into this life, maybe I could stay here long term?

I sighed and sat back down on the couch. That was, if Noah could forgive me for what I'd done, because from where I was standing, it didn't seem likely.

CHAPTER 10

NOAH

I was so angry, my fingers had shifted into claws, and I'd had to run out of the house so that Amy didn't see my loss of control. I didn't want the first glimpse of my wolf to scare her.

Another part of me was confused and annoyed because I didn't really know why I was so pissed. Sure, the existence of my child had been kept from me, and that needed to be dealt with, but surely berating Amy when she was right in the middle of owning up to her mistakes wasn't the way to go?

Especially after what had occurred last night.

I felt like a heel, talking in such a way to her this morning. If I wanted her to stay, I would have to figure out what the hell these feelings were that kept rising up inside me.

One moment I was as joyful as if I'd found my fated mate and our happy-ever-after, and the next I was rearing up in anger and fighting to keep my wolf from bursting out and howling at the proverbial moon.

I groaned as I ran a hand through my hair, pushing myself to continue to work, digging holes, building houses. Physical work that was meant to drive the voices from my head.

But it wasn't working. All I could see in my mind's eye was the way Amy writhed on the bed beneath me. How right it had felt to be near her, inside of her. Nothing had felt so perfect for me as last night. But every time she talked about staying, or going, the conversation only revolved around Trixie.

She never said anything about how she felt about *me*. Whether we should be together. That was what was pissing me off more than anything.

My wolf had yearned for her, for years. Literally. Had she thought about me once in that time? As more than Trixie's sperm donor?

I worked until my shoulders ached and sweat ran down my back. I wasn't interested in talking to anyone. Not Ronan, or Kit, or any of the other guys. I kept to myself until the bell rang to end the day.

There was relief in the sound. Time to go home. To my house. To my woman and child.

And yet she wasn't my woman. Not yet. But God, I wanted her to be.

I raised my hand in farewell to some of the guys I'd worked alongside today and started the walk home. I lifted my t-shirt to wipe the sweat off my face.

A high-pitched wolf whistle came from ahead of me. I glanced around only to see Lacey walking down the street swinging her hips.

Uh-oh.

"Hey lover," she called as she stepped closer.

"Excuse me?" I said, glancing around. "Who are you putting on a show for?"

She ignored my question and went up on her toes to kiss me.

I grimaced and pulled back, frowning at her. "What the hell are you trying to pull, Lacey?"

She shrugged. "Just offering you something I'm sure that little human isn't giving you. There's no way she could keep up with a wolf for strength or stamina. No way."

She grinned at me like she had already won the argument and I suppressed the urge to shudder.

"We haven't been lovers for a long time, Lacey, so I suggest you move on to the next guy on the list. I'm taken."

"Taken?" She crossed her arms over her breasts, pushing them up so her cleavage popped up above the neckline of her tank top. "You're not taken until you're mated, Noah, and I sure as hell can't see any new ring on you."

I clenched my jaw against the need to snap at her. "I've got a child, Lacey. That's more than enough commitment for me. So, just stay away, okay? I'm not interested."

I stormed off without looking back because I knew she would be throwing daggers with her expression. Lacey had never been the woman I wanted. I'd fought with her and gotten jealous when she'd been with others only because I wanted someone of my own.

Even if that person didn't fit me properly.

I knew who fit, with me and my wolf, and she'd left me. Now, she'd come back. So how hard was I going to fight to keep the right one around?

Very hard is the answer.

I jogged up the steps to my house and opened the front door.

And there was my little family, on the floor playing dolls. Amy was sitting cross legged on the rug, with Trixie's pink toys everywhere.

"Oh, hey!" she said, jumping to her feet. "I didn't know what time you were expected, so I only put dinner on a little while ago. Sorry."

I shook my head. "I'm not used to being waited on, Amy. You don't need to worry about that sort of stuff."

It was nice to come home to a kitchen smelling of beef and spices, though.

Trixie got to her feet and ran for me, her chubby little arms open.

"Hi!" I bent down to scoop her up.

She hummed at me, and I realized she had no name for me.

"Hey, Amy. What's Trixie going to call me?"

She walked over from the fridge, a beer and a bottle of water in hand. "What do you want her to call you?"

She handed me both, and I grabbed the water.

"Just this, thanks."

What had I called my dad? Just... Dad? "I haven't thought about it."

"Well, most of her friends from my mothers' group call their dads, Daddy, or some variation of it. But if you have another word, or something your family uses, go for it."

"Daddy." I liked the sound of that. My heart swelled and a grin split my face.

"Done," Amy said, like it was the simplest thing in the world. "That's what I'll call you when I'm talking to Trixie about you, and she'll pick it up soon enough, I'm sure. Now, dinner. How long do you want to wait to eat? Trixie kind of needs dinner soon, then I can get her to bed."

"Soon is great," I said, "though I need a shower. Can you take her and I'll just be ten minutes?"

I handed my little girl off to her mother and jogged through the house to the bathroom. I wanted to get back to my little family as soon as possible.

I washed, changed, then walked back down into the living room to be confronted by Lacey. In my house.

She was standing in the middle of the room looking angry, her eyebrows lowered and her cheeks flushed. The front door was shut and Amy stood beside her like they'd been talking. About what, I didn't want to imagine.

"What are you doing here?" I demanded.

Amy glanced away and down, avoiding looking at me as she walked away to the kitchen. Trixie came straight over to me, tears in her eyes.

"It's okay, sweetheart. Come here." I picked her up and she nestled into my chest. I glared at Lacey. "You're not welcome here."

Lacey laughed like I'd made a joke. "That's not what you usually say when I come over, Noah. What's wrong? Worried your little human will get jealous if we climb into bed together?"

My ribs squeezed tight around my heart, but I forged forward to the truth. "Amy, can you come here, please?"

Amy turned around and came back to me, though her arms were crossed and she stood too far away to touch. I needed to get this out in the open, and over and done with as soon as possible.

"Amy, this is Lacey. We dated on and off for years, while she was also doing whoever else she wanted in the pack. We aren't together now and haven't been for months. So don't let her get under your skin."

"Oh, don't be like that, Noah." Lacey grinned. "Just because this chick had your baby, doesn't mean you two need to be together. She'll never fit in around here. She needs to go home. And you need to stay here with your people."

I opened my mouth to retort, but Amy jumped in.

"Don't you have any self-respect?" she said, glaring at Lacey. "He's made it pretty damn clear he doesn't want you. So go home to whatever slop bucket you live in and leave my family alone."

Lacey whirled on Amy, her eyes shifting to her wolf.

"You're not a family." She spat. "You bore his bastard. Any woman could have done that."

"But *any* woman didn't," Amy all but growled back. "*I* did! So, fuck off and leave us alone."

I saw the shift in Lacey sooner than most would.

I jumped in front of my mate and shoved a whimpering Trixie at her. "Take her. Quick."

Lacey's humanity disappeared and a large black wolf stood in her place.

"My bedroom. Go," I managed to get out as my own wolf ripped through me.

Amy screamed, but I blocked out the pain that came from the sound. I needed to protect her first. I'd explain afterwards. I bared my teeth and growled at Lacey.

She launched at me.

I lifted my front paw and swiped at her face, hitting her square in the side of the head. She staggered sideways. I bore down on her, my teeth at her throat. She gnashed at me, fighting and scrabbling for purchase. Her claws scratched the floorboards, making a terrible screeching sound in the room.

She was a small wolf compared to me, so I didn't let up. Nothing had been more worth fighting for than the woman whom Lacey had just tried to attack. I tightened my jaw and pressed into her neck harder, tasting blood as my teeth cut into Lacey's throat.

Lacey dropped to the ground and lay still, her chest heaving with her frantic breath.

I made a final loud warning growl in my throat, then opened my jaws and backed away to allow her room to rise. If she tried to attack again, I'd rip a hole in her.

Lacey shifted back to human, now naked and practically sobbing on the floor. "It's not fair, Noah. You and I were always meant to be together. This wasn't the plan. *She* wasn't the plan."

I shifted back and grabbed for my ripped jeans, then threw them down again when I realized they were beyond salvageable. "You were never in my plans. Amy's my mate. She always has been."

"Your mate?" Lacey repeated, her eyes going wide and fearful. "No, she can't be."

I laughed and the sound was harsh even to my ears. "She is, and as soon as she agrees to be mine officially, you'll see the announcement go up around town. Now get out of here, before I do something we'll both regret."

Lacey grabbed her clothes and ran for the front door.

I turned around and marched down the corridor to where my bedroom door was closed.

Shit! What if the fight had scared Amy into leaving? That wasn't how I'd wanted my mate to meet my wolf.

I stepped closer and pressed my ear to the wood. I couldn't hear anything on the inside of the room, but hopefully she was still in there.

I didn't want to frighten her, so I called out just in case she needed the advance warning. "It's okay. It's all over."

The door flew open, and Amy's tear-stained face greeted me.

"Noah!" She threw herself into my arms and sobbed her heart out.

I wrapped my arms around her and held her tightly against my body. "It's okay, sweetheart. It's okay. I'll never let anyone hurt you. You're safe."

I consoled Amy while our daughter happily played on the floor, growling and barking with her little wolfy toy in her arms.

CHAPTER II
AMY

I'd never been so terrified in all my life. Not going into labor. Not the day I found out I was pregnant. Never.

When Lacey shifted before my eyes from human woman to a snarling black wolf, and Noah had told me to grab Trixie and run, I'd done what he asked. Who wouldn't have turned tail and fled when a massive wolf wanted my blood? But as soon as I was safe, or as safe as one could be behind a single wooden door, I became terrified for Noah. What if Lacey hurt him? What if he died? What would I do if something happened to him now that I'd finally found him again?

Then he'd knocked on the door and the knowledge that Noah

was alive and well flooded my highly stressed heart. I didn't know what to do with all the emotions pulsing through me. So, I burst into tears and cried all over him.

I cried like my heart was broken. Like someone had actually died. I cried for all the pain and misery, and shame and sadness that I'd dealt with over the past two years, walking this road alone when I should have been standing beside Noah the whole time.

Such a waste. So stupid.

"Come on," he said, "let's get you more comfortable."

He picked me up and took me further into the bedroom where our daughter was still playing on the floor with her wolf toy.

"The door," I managed to say, clinging to his shoulders. "Trixie."

I didn't want her wandering around the house, or out the front door. Not with those monsters hanging around.

He kicked shut the door behind us, then walked me over to the bed and sat down holding me.

"Are you okay?" he asked, stroking my hair.

I nodded, sniffing loudly. "Yes. I'm fine."

The silence stretched as he held me, and I realized suddenly that he was completely naked.

"Um." I sat up and wiped at my face. "Where are your clothes?"

He shrugged. "Shredded in the lounge. Unfortunately, shifting without warning has its disadvantages."

"What about Lacey?" I asked, images filling my head of the two of them rolling around on the lounge room floor naked. "Did she end up naked, too?"

Jealousy exploded inside of me. Not that they'd had time to fuck. It had felt like I'd been in that bedroom for hours, but I was pretty sure it had only been a few minutes.

He chuckled. "Does it worry you that much?"

You, rolling on the floor naked with another woman? In anger, perhaps, but anger was closely aligned with passion. I almost laughed, but instead I pressed my lips together, trying not to say something stupid, or mean. "I suppose not. It's just so strange to me."

He grinned. "You were more worried about the naked thing than the wolf thing?"

I shook my head. "No, that part was freaking terrifying, I admit. Part of me didn't believe you when you told me about it. Though…" This time I couldn't suppress the almost-hysterical laughter. "I guess I have to believe you, now."

I'd kind of hoped his explanation was a metaphor, or maybe like… a spirit animal. Anything but the truth, that he truly turned into an actual huge, hulking, wolf.

"Why would I lie?"

I huffed out a laugh while I traced patterns on his skin. "I didn't think you were actually lying, but… it didn't seem possible. In my world, where I come from, things like that are just myth and legend."

He sighed and pressed my head back to his chest. "What a mess this is."

I nodded, tears sliding down my cheeks at the relief of surviving such a stupid act of jealousy on Lacey's behalf. "And it's all my fault. I never should have left you in the first place."

If I hadn't left two years ago, then Lacey would never have been with Noah. The whole spiteful jealous show she'd just put on wouldn't have happened.

"No, you shouldn't have." Noah sighed, squeezing me tight. "But that can't be changed now. So we just need to work out a way to move forward, don't we?"

I nodded, feeling miserable. Those weren't the words of a man who really wanted to be with me. He was putting up with what I'd done, and who I was, for the sake of Trixie.

I had to ask. "You're never going to forgive me, are you?"

"It's not that I don't forgive you…" he said, then groaned. "It's just that…"

"Just, what?" I asked, sliding off his lap and sitting on the bed next to him. I handed him a pillow, which he looked at confused for a moment, before understanding dawned. He placed the pillow across his lap, hiding the enticing view.

Trixie was still happily sitting on the ground, playing with her wolf. She was growling and hissing like Lacey had.

I huffed a small laugh and nodded to Trixie. "She knows what sort of sounds wolves make now."

Noah didn't even crack a smile. "Yeah. Hopefully she wasn't scared."

"She's okay," I said, then assessed her again quickly. "She isn't clinging to me, or crying. I'd say she really is fine."

In fact, she hadn't seemed that perturbed at all. It was me that was a shaking mess.

Noah stood up. The pillow dropped away, and I tried not to look. Well, I looked a little. It was impossible not to, when his magnificent physique was right there in front of me. "Maybe I made the wrong call here."

"Which call was that?" I asked, hoping he didn't mean anything huge.

"Asking you two to move in here."

Oh, fuck. That was big.

Pain squeezed my heart. "What do you mean?"

Was he rejecting us now that I'd seen the truth and hadn't acted like I should have? Sure, he turned into a seriously scary-looking big gray wolf, but I could handle it. Couldn't I? He had come to our aid in an instant, and part of me knew he would never let any harm come to Trixie or me, if he could help it. I was just surprised, was all. Next time, I'd be better.

"I know that I don't exactly fit in here, but Trixie is going to need you guys. And Kara said I could talk to her human sister-in-law, Tammy. Maybe that will give us the answers we need about how Trixie's going to develop and... stuff."

Noah ran his hand over his jaw and through his hair.

"What wrong, Noah? Talk to me."

He was really worrying me now.

"I just think…. maybe Lacey was right, and we need to take you two back to town. I can't protect you twenty-four seven, and Trixie is still so young. Maybe's its better if you come back when she's older."

We'd been in danger for a few seconds and now he was pushing us away? That wasn't fair. It wasn't my fault I hadn't been raised to deal with wolves. Or the she-devil woman who had turned into one.

"Hang on a minute," I said, getting to my feet. "What about us?"

"What about… *us?*" Noah repeated. "You never even mention, *us*."

I did. I was sure I did.

"When I came back here," I began, worried that I'd put two and two together and come up with seven, "you said you wanted me. And Trixie."

He stared straight at me. "I did. And you haven't said once what you want."

"Oh." Maybe I was still trying to work out what I wanted. Or maybe I knew what I wanted, but didn't think it would ever be possible. "I haven't considered my own feelings in a long time. Trixie has been my whole world for so long."

Noah crossed his big arms over his beefy chest and stared at me. "Well, she has me now too. And I'm asking you, Amy, what do *you* want to happen, between us?"

He was putting me on the spot, and I didn't like it.

"I don't know," I hedged, because I didn't. I knew that we were fantastic in bed together, but could we build a life on that? "We haven't spent any real time together, so how can we judge?"

Noah spun away, growling.

I went straight to him, wrapping my arms around his naked waist from behind. "Please don't turn away from me. I'm trying. I promise. I just…"

He pushed away from me and went to his closet to pull out another set of clothes. He didn't speak as he tugged on black jeans and a gray shirt. "You just don't know. Yeah right. So, as always, I'm stuck in no man's land. The last one considered on your list of priorities."

Ouch. Arrow straight to the heart. "That's not true."

He did the last of his buttons on his shirt and glared at me. "Okay, then tell me right now. How do you feel about me? What do you want from me? A father for Trixie? A relationship between us? What?"

I covered my eyes with my hands, wanting to cry and run from the room. Everything had been too much to deal with. "Don't put me on the spot like that. It's not fair."

"No. What's not fair is that if you were a wolf, you'd know what this is. What we are to each other. And you wouldn't be afraid of it."

I dropped my hands from my eyes and glared back at him. "Are you serious right now? You're saying that it would be better if I was a wolf? Well, I'm so sorry that I'm not some snarling, nasty beast like Lacey. I'm only a poor, weak, stupid human woman who doesn't know anything about anything."

Noah's eyes widened until he narrowed his gaze back at me. "Nasty? Snarling beast? Is that how you see me?"

"Well, ah…" Of course, I didn't see him that way. I'd been talking about Lacey, not Noah. Lacey, who'd just tried to attack me and my child.

"I suppose that's how you're going to see our daughter too when she shifts for the first time." Noah sounded more like he was talking to himself than me, and there was a note of sadness in his tone that did not bode well.

"No… that's not what I meant. Don't be ridiculous."

"Ridiculous?" Noah marched over to the bedroom door and threw it open. "I was right. You need to go back to town and be with your own people."

I hurried over to our daughter and scooped her up into my arms. "But I came here for help with her. I still don't have any answers."

Noah twisted his head away, an angry muscle in his jaw tight and ticking away.

Then he swiveled back. "Okay. We'll get you the answers you came for. Who did Kara say to ask for advice?"

"Um." I bit my lip, searching my memory for the name. I was so flustered by Noah and this whole situation, that I couldn't remember. Then it came back to me. "Her sister-in-law. Tammy, she said."

He nodded. "I'll go talk to Kara. There's food in the fridge. You do dinner and all your nightly routine stuff with Trixie and I'll be back when I can. Don't wait up."

He marched off toward the front door and I hurried after him, Trixie grunting and trying to get down from my arms so that she could get to her father.

"That's it?" I called out, shocked he was leaving so abruptly after such a heavy discussion.

He opened the door and turned back to look at me. "What do you mean?"

"You're just leaving us? Right now?"

He heaved a heavy sigh. "I'm not leaving you. I'm going to find someone who can help you."

"But we haven't finished talking." The wounds were all broken open and weeping, and he just wanted to walk away? This was when we needed to push through the uncomfortable parts and get to the other side.

He finally muttered, "I think you've said enough."

"And you haven't said anything," I shot back. "You haven't told me how *you* feel, or what *you* want."

His face went blank and cold. "I've told you everything, Amy. And if you can't hear what I'm saying, or feel what I feel, then we're not fated mates like I thought."

Fated mates? What did he mean? But before I could ask, he walked away, shutting the door behind him.

Trixie cried out as I set her on the ground. She sobbed as she ran for the door, "Dada. Dada!"

"Oh baby," I cried, tears sliding down my cheeks. "Daddy will be back soon. Don't worry."

He'd missed her first words for him, and that broke me. He'd missed so much, and if we couldn't sort out this shit, he would miss a hell of a lot more.

I cuddled Trixie into my chest as she sobbed and I cried. So much hurt, and rejection and pain. On every side.

"It's okay, baby. It's okay. Mommy will find a way out of this."

But hells if I knew the way right now. I got my tears under control and focused on my daughter. Her needs were all that mattered. I made her dinner, gave her a quick wash down with baby wipes, and put her to bed.

Then I sat on the couch with a cup of tea and waited for my baby-daddy to come home.

CHAPTER 12
NOAH

Walking away from my home, and my mate, and my daughter, was one of the hardest things I'd done to date. But I had to, or I'd lose control of myself, and perhaps my wolf. I was so angry I could barely speak.

I could feel my teeth shifting in my mouth, and the heat of my body ratchet up to the point I had to breathe deep and force my shifter back down inside.

I had a job to do. So instead of running into the forest like I really needed to, I found my Alpha and his mate at home. They invited me in and quickly agreed to help me by getting Tammy to speak to Amy.

"I can call her tonight if you want?" Kara offered. "Ask when you can drop by."

"Yes please, as soon as possible," I said. "I'll drive Amy and Trixie over tomorrow morning if that suits them and Tammy."

Kara grabbed her phone. "Back in a bit."

She stepped into the hall.

Ronan offered me a beer and we sat down on the couch. I was jittery as all hell.

"So," Ronan said casually, taking a sip of his beer, "things not going quite to plan?"

I snorted, pushing my hair off my face. "It's a fucking farce, is what it is. I can't believe I thought a human was my mate."

I had to be wrong about that. Things were not meant to be this hard.

"What makes you think she isn't?" Ronan asked quietly.

I groaned and took a sip of beer. "It's meant to be easy, isn't it? Natural. Fated mates just fit together, without any effort at all. And yet, with Amy, everything is a fight. A slog. I feel like I'm walking on eggshells every time I speak... my moods are all over the place. It shouldn't... I don't know. This is not how I thought it would be with her. If she really is my fated mate, why is it this hard? Not only for me, but for her, too? I can see she's not happy with how it is with us, either. Maybe I was wrong. Maybe she isn't my mate."

Instead of nodding and agreeing with me, as I expected, Ronan chuckled, setting his beer down on the coffee table. He leaned back and folded his hands behind his head, studying me. "You think everything with Kara has been easy from the start? She left me, ran off home. Remember?"

"Yeah, but—"

"But nothing. Relationships, even when they're fated, are messy. There's always fights and mistakes made along the way."

I groaned. "Yeah, but you two sorted it out pretty fast. I don't know how Amy and I are going to get past everything, Ronan. There's too much history. I thought I could just forget what she did and move on. Forgive her for lying to me for so long and keeping Trixie away."

"And you can't forgive that?"

"I don't know."

It wasn't that easy, to just decide I could or couldn't forgive something. And it didn't help that I still didn't know if Amy even wanted me at all. She hadn't admitted to having any feelings for me in a current context, and until she did, we were at a stale mate, with me wanting her for life, and her too afraid to come forward and be honest—one way or the other.

Or maybe that was the problem. She *didn't* actually want me at all, and hadn't said anything because she was afraid of hurting my feelings and making me feel rejected, or some bullshit like that? That would make sense. Maybe she'd only fallen into bed with me last night because the poor thing had been so starved for sex. I mean, she'd practically said that. Lust and forever love were too entirely separate things.

Maybe... I dropped my head into my hands and rubbed my face. My thoughts felt tied up in knots. I didn't know what I was thinking, anymore, let alone being capable of figuring what Amy wanted. Or didn't want.

"Fuck." I sighed, the weight of defeat crushing the hope in my chest. "I think I need to let her go. For all our sakes."

Kara walked back into the room at that moment, phone in hand. "Tammy said you can bring Amy and Trixie over in the morning. The baby's down for the night, otherwise she'd come straight over now."

I stood up and smiled at my Alpha's mate, feeling a sense of relief.

"Thanks, Kara, I appreciate that." I stretched my back, pulling my arms up and over my head. "I think I need a run. I feel... restless."

It was more than that; my wolf was practically on the verge of shifting. He was always there, vibrating at the edges of my control. I'd shifted only a few hours ago to fight Lacey, but the adrenaline was still zinging through my system and I had to work it off.

I needed a run. A proper one.

"I'd offer to come with you, but my mate has requested we go to bed early," Ronan said, with a boastful grin.

To make it even more obvious what he was talking about, Kara blushed prettily and whacked Ronan on the arm.

I laughed and opened the front door, jealous of their easy, happy relationship. "Thanks again for your help."

"I'll come with you in the morning, if that's okay?" Kara said, rubbing her belly. "I'd like to catch up with my brother, and it'll be easier to navigate if I show you the best road there."

"That would be much appreciated," I said.

I walked down the front steps of their house and started to unbutton my shirt. "Do you mind if I leave my clothes here, and I'll come back after my run?"

"Not at all. Go for it," Ronan said.

"Isn't Amy expecting you back?" Kara called out.

I shrugged. "She's got Trixie. She doesn't seem to need anyone else."

I took off my shirt and pulled off my jeans. My wolf rose up inside me and took over, making my human side disappear. The feelings that came with the shift were fantastic. My mind slipped away from everything, the worries, the stress, and the pain.

In its place was power, strength, and a hunger for life that wasn't present in human form.

I dug my paws into the dirt and took off, running through town, across the back streets and into the forest. The sun was just dropping from the sky. Rabbits bolted out of my way, and I could sense a deer nearby as well. Senses were always heightened during the shift. Hearing and smell in particular, as well as physical speed, were at their peak.

But I didn't want to hunt. I just wanted to run. To feel free and happy. Something I hadn't felt in too long to think about.

I reached halfway to the main town when I slowed down.

Something tugged at my heart to stop, and I did. I wanted to go forward, but it was like the ground had rooted me to the spot.

I had to go home to my mate and child.

The run home was slower, as I carried a heavier heart. My wolf was certain that Amy was my mate, and yet the same woman had left me after our first night together. She would never have sought me out even now, if it wasn't for Trixie's wolf-like characteristics.

It tore at my heart, and my pride, that she didn't feel the same way I did. But could I expect her to, when she was human? Maybe it wasn't the same for humans as it was for shifters. Maybe she didn't have this aching certainty in her heart—in her *soul*—the way I did, that we were destined for one another if we wanted it.

I reached Ronan's house when it was full dark, changed into my clothes, and walked back to my house. I was pretty sure I'd missed more than dinner. I would have missed Trixie's bath time, sleep time, and perhaps even Amy going to bed.

There were no lights on when I arrived home. I snuck in quietly, locking the door behind me.

Dinner was sitting on the kitchen table, a cold stew in a large bowl. I had no appetite, but heated the meal in the microwave and ate it anyway. Amy had gone to the trouble to cook, and the stew was tasty once reheated, salted well with lots of big chunks of potatoes and pumpkin along with tender meat.

It should have made me happy to see signs that she was trying to settle in, and that she possibly wanted to stay with me. But all I saw were the advantages of living with a woman who was used to caring for herself and her child.

Once I'd cleaned up, I snuck by the spare bedroom. The door was shut. I paused there for so long I forgot what I was waiting for. Did I want to talk to Amy about what had happened tonight between us? Probably not.

Did I want her to come out and say goodnight? No. That might not end well for either of us.

Was she even in there? Or would I find her asleep in my bed? *Our bed.*

With a heart that was a little too happy at the prospect that I would once again be sleeping alongside her warm body, I crept up the hallway to my room.

When I pushed open the door and found the bedroom empty, the disappointment was crushing and far outweighed the expectations I should have had. I'd walked out on her after a fight. After her life had been threatened, by a woman who turned into a wolf in front of Amy. Then she'd seen me change. Confirmation that the father of her child was not human, after all.

Why would she sleep with me?

I slunk into my room and shut the door, had a quick shower, and crawled into bed.

Was Amy asleep in the spare bedroom? Or was she wide awake and aching with loneliness and confusion, like me?

I slid between the sheets. My wolf wasn't happy, and neither was I.

What the hell was I going to do about this situation now?

Should I fight to spend time with them? Should I keep them here while we worked out the best way forward?

Or should I let Amy go? Back to her own life in the city? Try and co-parent together, like so many other parents did—parents who were not together, but still shared a child or children. I could do weekends with my daughter. Was that really a life for a wolf like me? Especially with the way I felt about Amy.

I closed my eyes and tried to get some sleep, even though my chest was tight and I was the closest to shedding a tear I'd been in my adult life.

Everything about this just felt wrong, but at least we had some kind of a plan. We would talk to Kara and Tammy tomorrow morning, and hopefully another human woman would give some clarification to the situation. For Amy, and possibly for me.

Ronan's words stuck with me though, casting a little light in the darkness. He'd said that the road of a relationship, even with a fated mate, wasn't always smooth.

I clung to that thought through the long, lonely night.

CHAPTER 13
AMY

I had a truly shit night's sleep. Not because Trixie woke me up, or cried through the night. She was a little angel.

It was me. My mind whirled. I couldn't think anything nice or positive to concentrate on, and a strange type of depression chased me, even in my dreams when I did finally drift off.

After waiting hours for Noah, I'd gone to bed angry. So, I'd been awake when Noah had finally gotten home. I'd heard him enter the house, eat the dinner I'd cooked, then stand outside my bedroom door. I'd been so mad at him for staying away, I was half ready to jump up out of bed and yell in his face if he opened the door to check on me. But he never did.

After what felt like an eternity of holding my breath and lying super still on the mattress, I'd heard him sigh heavily and walk down to his own bedroom, all without even checking if I was awake or not. Thanks to that frustrating moment, I'd tossed and turned for most of the night.

When I woke up the next morning, I was exhausted and wanted to sleep the day away.

"Mama, Mama," Trixie called from her pack-and-play.

I didn't move a muscle, hoping she would lie down and go back to sleep if she thought I was still out for the count.

Instead, the creaking of the thin mattress as she jumped up and down sounded. She was obviously excited to see me in a bed in her room.

I lifted my head and glanced down at her. "Agh, sweetheart. Please tell me you're going to have at least two naps today. I'm gonna need them!"

I hauled myself up out of bed and reached into the crib for her. She looked just as gorgeous and sparkly as ever, with her beautiful blue eyes and clear, pale skin.

"Are you really going to turn into one of those wolves one day?" I asked her, even now doubting the truth of those words. "Because if you do, I'm going to be the odd one out around here."

I crept to the door, opened it, and went out to the kitchen to make her a bottle.

I'd been shocked by the transformations I'd seen yesterday between Noah and Lacey. And yet, despite how vicious and nasty they'd seemed when facing each other down, I'd known that Noah was only protecting us. That fact was strangely comforting. Noah had shown that he would defend us against any enemy, including his own kind. Not to mention he would clearly be able to kick any human's ass, that was for sure.

I made Trixie a bottle, put on the coffee maker, and took her back to bed with me to cuddle with her. I lay with my head on the pillow and stared at the beautiful daughter I'd created. With Noah. I stroked her cheek and cupped her little ear, enjoying the few minutes of quiet that we had together in the morning, before the day really started and the whirlwind of life took over.

Trixie finished her bottle, handed the empty thing to me, then rolled over to sit up. She was so independent now, so big. My little baby was mostly gone.

There was a knock at the door, and I twisted around to look. "Hello?"

The door opened and Noah peek into the room, his blue eyes dark and sad. "Morning."

"Good morning."

Trixie slid off the bed and ran for him.

"Dada," she chanted, and Noah laughed as he scooped her up.

"She's saying *Dada* already."

I swallowed hard against the lump of emotions in my throat. "Yeah, she is. She's very clever."

He nodded, wrapping his arms around her. "I'll make us some breakfast, then we've gotta get going."

"Oh yeah? Where are we going?" I asked, getting to my feet and reaching for my bags with all our clean clothes.

"When I went to see Ronan and Kara last night, we organized to head over to Tammy's today. Kara thought you might be able to ask her sister-in-law more questions about cross-mixed babies, since she has one, too."

Relief filled me at the news. That sounded like a great idea. I took out diapers for Trixie and got our things ready for the day. "That sounds perfect, thank you."

Noah handed our daughter back to me, then pointed his thumb at the kitchen. "I'll get on the food, then we can go."

"Great."

Noah left without another word, and a huge hole ripped inside my heart. What little friendship we'd built over the last few days had been stripped away, leaving nothing but the burning awkwardness usually felt between exes. That feeling made everything seem insurmountable. The wolf thing. The single mom thing. The fact that I'd lied to him for so long. Everything.

Suddenly, my life was too hard and I couldn't see a way to fix it.

Trixie tugged at my leg and held out her clean diaper for me. My clever girl. I sighed and took a slow, measured breath. This little one depended on me, so there was no falling in a hole today. Not tomorrow either.

Maybe later. When she was all grown up and capable of taking care of herself.

"Okay, baby. Let's get you clean and dressed."

Once we were both ready to face the day, I wandered out into the living room and was met with a simple yet yummy-looking breakfast.

"That looks great. Thank you."

Noah glanced at the table. "I can't cook much, but I can chop."

He'd cut up strawberries, apples, bananas, and pears. There was yoghurt and toast and bread rolls.

"It's perfect. Thank you."

My heart lifted at seeing him trying so hard with us once more.

He handed me a coffee, his face as quiet and still as the surface of a mill pond. Equally as unreadable. "Let's eat."

We sat down and ate our food, Trixie passing between us to eat snatches of each of our breakfasts. A bite of toast from me, a piece of banana from Noah. It was lovely and gave my foolish heart hope that this is how things could be between us, if we could only figure out a way forward.

When we were done, having not talked about anything other than how cute Trixie was, we cleaned up and packed the car in virtual silence.

"I'll sit in the back with Trixie if you don't mind driving," I said to Noah, throwing him the keys.

He caught them, surprise in his face. "You sure?"

"Yeah, of course. Kara should sit in the front with you since she'll need the leg room. Plus, she can help navigate. I don't even know where we're going."

And I didn't care. I'd drive clear across the country and back again if it got me answers about Trixie's health.

We hopped in the car with me in the backseat with the baby, then Noah drove us over to a huge house at the top of the hill.

"Whoa. So that's the Alpha's house?" I asked.

"Yep. It's big, isn't it?"

I nodded. "Huge."

Kara waddled out, a grin on her face. "How are you guys this morning?"

"Fine, thanks," we both said, as she climbed in. Then, off we drove.

"How far is this place?" I asked no one in particular.

Kara twisted around to grin at me. "Oh, it's about an hour's drive on the main roads, but I know a few tricks to get there faster."

We drove through the forest, up hills and around corners, Noah heading wherever Kara pointed. If I'd been worried about my safety with these two people, then the fact that we were driving into the wilderness with no signs of life would definitely have sent up red flags.

But I didn't have anything to worry about with these two, so I dismissed the silly thought. A pregnant woman, and a man who loved my daughter, weren't going to cause any issues in that regard.

I just sat back and listened to them chatter about the pack while I entertained Trixie with food, toys, and my phone when she got too restless for anything else.

When we arrived at another small town, with gorgeous little houses and developed roads, I sighed. "Wow. This place is nice."

"Yeah," Kara said softly. "I grew up here, and although we've gone through a few rough times, it's a great town. If we have time to stop and see Allara, I think you'd really like her."

"Who's Allara?" I asked.

"My best friend."

"The Alpha," Noah elaborated.

"You mean the Alpha's mate?" I asked, assuming that Allara was the wife of the Alpha, the same way Kara was Ronan's mate.

"No, she's the Alpha," Kara said. "She was the only child of our old Alpha, and even though Jaime challenged her, she won in a death match."

"Wow." That definitely sounded like a woman I wanted to know. Only, *death* match? That sounded pretty scary.

Kara chuckled. "Yeah, she's pretty kick ass."

No kidding.

We drove up to a small house, and a smiling woman walked out the front door holding a baby girl in her arms.

"Tammy!" Kara cried, stepping out of the car and waddling over to meet the woman.

I unclipped Trixie from her car seat. My daughter was dying to get out, thrashing about and crying as I released her.

"I'll get her," Noah said, coming around to Trixie's side of the car and opening the door.

"Oh. Okay. Thanks." What else could I say? That *I* wanted to get her, like I always did? That would sound petty.

Instead, I grabbed my bag and Trixie's things and walked up toward the woman who looked as human as me. And Kara. I would never have been able to pick Tammy out as being a human when Kara wasn't. On the surface, they both seemed just like every other human woman I'd ever known.

"Hi," I said, smiling at Tammy and the little girl in her arms. "I'm Amy."

"Hey! I'm Tammy and this is Claire."

Tammy had a strong, sure voice, and a sweet face. She was also slightly more curvy than the wolf shifters I'd seen in Noah's town.

"Hi Claire." I waved at the little one, and she gave me a shy smile. "Oh God, she's beautiful."

Tammy groaned. "Well, she might look cute, but she kept me up half the night for God knows what reason, so come on in and let's have some coffee. I apologize in advance if I'm grouchy."

I laughed as I followed her. "Been there. Done that."

Kara hung by the door, but didn't come in. "Hey Tammy, do you mind if I go say hi to Allara?"

"Of course not. Go for it. I think she might be at the council building this morning."

Kara snuck off and left me alone with Tammy, Noah and the two little ones.

Tammy went to the kitchen and turned on the coffee maker. "So, guys. What's going on?"

I glanced over at Noah, who was still holding Trixie and seemed to have gone mute. "Well... I've got a few questions, if you don't mind."

"Yeah? About what?"

"About, you know, babies of wolf shifters and humans, and what it's like to live out here when you're not... one of them."

Tammy popped her daughter in a highchair and grinned at me. "Have you seen Noah shift yet? How fucking scary is it, right?"

"Seeing as how he shifted in the lounge room to protect me and Trixie from another wolf—a woman—who wanted to attack us, I'd say it was pretty fucking scary."

I glanced toward Noah, who was avoiding my gaze and didn't see that I'd softened my words with a grin. I turned back to Tammy, whose mouth had dropped open, and was unable to stop the laugh that bubbled up and out of my throat. "It was kind of surreal, actually, to witness that shift. I'm still not sure I've assimilated it all."

"No kidding," Tammy said, with a quick head shake.

Noah shot me a sharp look when I laughed, and though he still didn't say anything, something about the line of his jaw seemed to relax a notch.

He sat on the floor with Trixie and let her rummage through Claire's toy box.

"Well, have a seat," Tammy said to me, gesturing to one of the dining chairs that surrounded the nice wooden table. "Sounds like we've got lots to talk about."

CHAPTER 14
AMY

I thought about what to ask, and a hundred questions popped into my head. Then I realized that my first questions had to be about Trixie. After all, that was the main reason I'd sought Noah out, wasn't it?

"Well, I suppose I should ask, how was your labor with Claire?"

Tammy blinked at me, and I blinked back. Yeah, that wasn't what I'd thought would come out of my mouth either, first up, but here we were.

Tammy ran her hands over the table in front of her as though she were nervous. "Okay, weird place to start, but I guess it was good. I had her here, at home. It wasn't fun. I screamed the place down. But no drugs, no stitches, no intervention. Was a dream labor compared to some of my friends in the city. Why?"

Wow. That sounded like heaven in comparison to me, and not what I'd been expecting her to say.

"I thought maybe the wolf-human mix might cause a harder birth. That's all."

"Not for me," she said, then grinned. "But I've had these lovely childbearing hips my whole life."

She wiggled on her seat and her breasts wobbled as she moved.

I smiled at her openness. She had a lovely curvy figure.

"You're perfect," I said shyly.

"You had a hard time with Trixie's birth?" she asked.

I could feel Noah's eyes on me, but I didn't want to look his way. We hadn't really talked about that. To be honest, we hadn't really talked about a lot of stuff, yet.

"I did. Once I found out about Noah, I was kind of hoping it might have been the wolf-human genetic mix." I shrugged. "But it might have just been me."

Which was what I'd always assumed until I found out Noah wasn't human.

"Or the medical intervention," Tammy said with a frown. "How bad was it?"

I shrugged. "Almost died, but you know. I didn't."

Noah jumped up to stand beside me. "You almost died?"

I glanced up at him, my chest tight with strain. "Yeah. They needed forceps to get her out because she got stuck, and they tore something that caused me to almost bleed out. But they stopped the bleeding, got me into surgery, and I got a few pints of someone else's blood in a transfusion."

I tried to make light of the situation; after all I'd survived it. Other women hadn't.

Noah's jaw tightened, and his gaze hardened as though he was angry.

He shouldn't be. It wasn't like it was his fault.

"Oh my God," Tammy said, drawing my attention back to her. "You must be terrified to have another."

"Oh, I have no plans for any more," I said, and then it hit me.

Oh, my God. I had unprotected sex with Noah. Again.

My gaze shot up to Noah and he stared right back as if the same thought had just crossed his mind.

Oh, crap. Not again.

"Well, maybe a C-section next time?" Tammy said, breezing on with the conversation. "Not that I've heard that's any better, but at least it's more controlled."

I nodded. "That's what the doctors said at the time." *What day am I on in my cycle? Ten? Eleven? Shit! I don't know.*

Was it really possible to get two for two?

"Anything else you want to know?" Tammy asked, glancing between us.

Yes, I thought. *A million things. But I don't know where to start.*

Noah walked off to play with Trixie, as if wanting to give us space, and I shook myself. I could deal with that issue later.

Focus.

I swallowed hard and forged on. "Trixie is already showing wolf-like signs. She howls in her sleep, and her eyes shift color too. Do you know what the likelihood of her being a full shifter, is?"

The words came out robotically, as my head spun with the possibilities. What would I do if I was pregnant again? Could I do another baby on my own? How would Noah feel about this one?

If it happened again, I would have to be up front and honest with Noah from the beginning. I owed it to him, and to the child. If there was another one.

"To be honest, I don't know. No one's really talked to me about it. I'd say, just assume she will and educate her accordingly. And if she doesn't, well, you can deal with that then." Tammy took a sip of her coffee, then went to the cupboard and pulled out a container of biscuits. "Are you planning on staying with the Northwood Pack? Will Trixie grow up knowing about the wolves?"

"We haven't really decided on that yet," I said, glancing at Noah, who wasn't looking at me. He was squatting down next to Trixie, looking at the her while she played her little games.

I wasn't lying though; we hadn't even discussed that topic, let alone come to any decisions.

"Well, that will really determine how much she knows and is comfortable with," Tammy said. She stared at me long and hard.

I tilted my head at her. "What's up?"

She turned in her chair. "Hey, Noah. Can I chat with Amy for a bit by herself? Is that okay?"

Noah picked up Trixie and walked over to us. "Yeah, sure. I'll just take Trixie for a walk."

Tammy jumped to her feet.

"I'll walk you out." She looked at me. "Can you watch Claire for a second? I'll be right back."

"Yeah. Of course." I slid closer to the little girl and handed her one of the toys that had been out of reach.

My ears strained to listen to what Noah and Tammy were saying, but I could barely even hear whispering. Either they'd walked too far away for me to hear, or they had ultra-sonic whispering skills.

"What do you think they're saying?" I said to Claire, then sighed because I was hopeless.

I forced myself to concentrate on Claire, enjoying her tiny hands and smile. Then Tammy walked back in.

"I think I've got the lay of the land now. So, tell me what's going on with you." Tammy sat down again opposite me and grabbed a cookie with the air of a woman on a mission.

"I'm not sure what you mean."

Wasn't I the one who was meant to ask *her* questions?

Tammy took a sip of coffee from her large mug, then gestured at me with her hand. "How are you dealing with the whole... wolf thing?"

"Which bit?" I asked with a nervous laugh. "The fact that Noah is one, or the fact that my daughter might become one?"

Tammy grinned. "Well, both."

I worried my bottom lip with my teeth for a moment before answering. "I don't really know. It's scary and still seems totally surreal, but I suppose I'm okay with it. I mean, it could be worse, right?"

Even as I said the words, I was thinking, not sure how, but there had to be worse scenarios.

Tammy nodded. "Think about all the kids that inherit syndromes that cause disabilities. As a wolf shifter, Trixie will have a lot of advantages that we humans don't have."

"Like what?"

"Like speed and strength, not to mention an awesome metabolism. And their ability to heal is off the charts."

"Really? I didn't know about any of those things." Some of those sounded very cool.

Tammy cackled. "Yeah, that's because Noah's finding it hard enough just to think clearly around you, without sitting down and explaining all the wolf concepts."

Before I could jump in with a question about what she meant, she continued on. "Plus, they don't really think about all the cool things they've got that we don't. It's only us that notice the differences because we're not wolves. They pretty much take all those things for granted."

I inhaled slowly through my nose, conflicted in which way to take the conversation. "You, um, seem totally fine with it all."

"I am," Tammy said, and her tone was truly happy. "A wolf shifter mate is the best husband, or boyfriend, or whatever you want to call it. They're insanely loyal, and if you're lucky enough to be fated mates with one, then they'll never leave you. Never look at another woman again, no matter how old or chubby you get. And turns out it's the same for me, even though I'm human. Once someone commits to their fated mate, whether it is two shifters, or a human and a shifter, they will never want or need another partner."

Tammy picked up another biscuit and chomped on it, the ordinary action belying her momentous words.

Was she serious?

"What actually is a fated mate? Is it like... a soul mate?" That sounded awesome.

Tammy nodded. "That's a good description. Some of the wolves say they feel a special attraction to their fated mate. It's a person who is absolutely perfect for them, and because of that, they can't be with anyone else. That's what it was like for me and Jason, and Allara and Reid."

"And Kara and Ronan?" I added, thinking of those two and suddenly knowing exactly what she was talking about.

She nodded with a grin. "You've seen them together?"

"Yeah, there's this... happiness to them. A glow. I can't quite put it into words."

Tammy placed her elbow on the table and leaned on her hand. "That's the bond. With Jason and I it was a bit harder to deal with. Obviously, not being a wolf shifter, I didn't understand how intensely Jason felt about me. Or how hard he struggled with the fact that I was human."

"What do you mean?" I asked as she stood up to pick up Claire, who had begun to fuss.

Tammy hoisted her baby up into her arms and popped a pacifier in her mouth. "I mean, the wolves don't really like dating outside the pack. In the past it has brought with it too many issues, which was part of the reason Jason didn't really want to date me." She shrugged. "But what can I say? When it's meant to be, it's meant to be."

"I wish it was like that for me and Noah," I said with a sigh, then realized I'd said that out loud. I slammed my hands over my mouth. "I'm sorry. I didn't actually mean to say that."

Tammy laughed. "You and Noah need to talk this thing out. You've already lost two years when you could have been together and deliriously happy. Do you really wanna lose more time?"

I frowned at her. "You think Noah still wants to be with me?"

"Not sure what's changed from me talking to him ten minutes ago," she said matter-of-factly.

I stared at her in wonder. Had Noah really told her that he wanted me? No, he couldn't have. I frowned. That didn't match up with what he'd told me.

"He said it was better I leave. That I was safer in town, away from the wolves."

And any psycho exes that had the ability to bite my head off. Quite literally.

She shrugged. "Maybe you are. I don't know. But what I do know is that these guys are insanely protective and would rather cut off their own right arm, than see you fall in harm's way. So even if it kills him, Noah will send you away if he thinks you're better off without him."

Even if it kills him? Is it really like that, for Noah? Tears gathered in my eyes and began to block up my nose. I opened my mouth to speak, then closed it and shook my head instead. Nope. Couldn't talk.

Tammy sighed, juggling the baby from one hip to the other. "Amy, look, being out here can be rough, and leaving your whole world behind... yeah, that takes a bit to get used to as well. But these men... if they love you, they will move heaven and earth for you. That sort of love is worth any sacrifice, in my view."

I swallowed hard and brushed the tears off my check. "How will I know if he loves me like that or not?"

I didn't know if he could ever really love me in the way she had spoken about. Love like that involved trust, and that would mean he would need to forgive me for what I'd done.

Tammy grabbed a box of tissues and handed them to me. "You really need to just sit down and talk to him, Amy. He'll be honest with you, as long as you're honest with him."

"But I am honest with him!" I told her. "I try to tell him every-thing now."

She frowned. "Well, he thinks you're holding something back. About why you left. And I can't tell you much more, because we only chatted for a few minutes, but if you want to save this relationship, you've gotta tell him everything. No holds barred. I mean, you have a child together. And if you do love Noah, then full honesty is the only thing that might save this situation."

If I do love Noah? My heart jiggled in a strange erratic beat. Tammy was right. It *was* time for full honesty. With Noah, and with myself.

I nodded and wiped up my tears, just as a knock sounded on the door.

It was Kara and Allara, ready to chat and do a meet and greet. I put on my happy face and tried to focus on the women in front of me, but in the back of my head my thoughts were spinning.

From what Tammy was saying, *I* was the one standing in the way of my happily ever after with Noah.

But what did he need to hear for us to move forward?

CHAPTER 15
NOAH

I played with Trixie in the woods, enjoying the sunshine and her bubbly company. She was such a content child. She giggled and chatted away in her own little language, radiating happiness.

I'd had no idea, until Amy turned up with Trixie, that being a dad could feel so damn wonderful.

What would I do when they returned to town without me? My heart sank at the thought of not being with them. Either of them. Trixie had wriggled her way into my heart the moment I saw her. Just like her mom.

My woman. My child. My family.

Could I simply continue my life as a bachelor? A single wolf whose mate lived an hour away?

No, not my mate. I shook the thoughts from my head. Just because my wolf thought of her that way, didn't mean it was true.

I was just walking back to town with Trixie snuggled in my arms when Allara found us.

"Hey Noah," she called out. "I think the girls are ready to leave."

"Yeah. Cool. Coming."

Had Amy found any of the answers she'd been searching for? And did that mean she now felt safe to take Trixie back to town and away from me until she was older?

Most wolf shifters didn't start their transitions until they hit puberty. I hadn't told Amy because I wanted to keep her around. Now, I should probably reassure her that Trixie wouldn't have any issues for ten years or so. Hopefully. I didn't know anything about what happened with a half human, but I had to assume the shifter traits were likely to be diluted rather than amplified.

When I got back to the car, Kara and Amy were already packed and ready to go.

"Trixie really needs a nap, and she'll fall asleep in the car on the way home," Amy said, reaching out for our daughter.

There was a look in her eye that I couldn't read as she studied me. It made my stomach wobble. I nodded, pretending calm, and loving the way Amy said 'home' when she described my place. It was probably just a slip of the tongue, but even so, it warmed me for a long moment.

I said my goodbyes to Allara and Tammy, and then hopped in the car.

"Did you get the information you needed?" I asked Amy as we began the drive back to our pack.

"Mostly," she said quietly, fussing over Trixie in the back seat and not meeting my eye in the rear view mirror.

We didn't talk much for the drive home, all three of us deep within our own thoughts. We dropped Kara back at her house, and she staggered up her front stairs, holding her back and her belly at the same time.

"Is she okay?" I asked Amy, frowning as Kara finally disappeared inside. "Is she meant to look like that?"

She didn't respond at first, then said, "Probably just some sciatica. Happens when you sit for too long. She'll be okay, but I can check on her tomorrow."

"Tomorrow?" I repeated, twisting around in my seat to look at her. "You're staying?"

She stared at me with an unreadable expression. "I'd like to. Can we talk about it at home?"

This time the use of the word home seemed to be deliberate, and I couldn't stop the wave of hope that swept through my chest.

"Yeah, of course. Let's go."

I drove back to my place as fast as it was safe to do so, and Amy carefully picked up the sleeping Trixie and carried her inside. I held the bedroom door open and watched her place our daughter in her crib. Trixie kept her eyes closed, and she cuddled into her blanket and wolf toy with a little sigh of what sounded like contentment.

Amy snuck out and shut the door, grinning with relief. "She doesn't always transfer well, so you must have done a good job of wearing her out."

"I didn't do much. Truth be told, she kept me going, with all her energy. It was probably all the fresh air as well." Of which we had lots, being out in the forest.

Nothing like town.

"Can we chat now?" Amy asked, her dark eyes big and open.

My stomach twisted into knots. I couldn't tell where this was headed. What was she going to tell me? "Sure."

We walked back into the lounge room and sat down opposite each other on the two couches surrounding the coffee table. I stared at her, waiting for her to begin. She wanted this discussion, so I was going to let her lead.

Besides, my throat was closed over with nervous tension, so I needed a moment before I could get any coherent words out.

She shifted on her spot on the couch, and cleared her throat with a cough. "I really enjoyed meeting Tammy today. It was really good of you to organize that and take me over there. Thank you."

I nodded, then had to do a little throat clearing of my own. Finally, I felt I could trust my voice not to betray my nerves. "Sure. Anything in particular you learnt that you want to talk about?"

She bit her lip, then jerked her head in a nod. "Yes. Tammy told me that wolves have fated mates."

I froze. *Shit.* I hadn't wanted Tammy to tell Amy that. "Yeah, some of us do."

"Do you have one?" she asked, staring at me intently.

Fuck. Talk about being backed into a corner.

I straightened up on my cushion. "Well... that's still to be decided."

She frowned at me. "What do you mean? I thought you just... knew."

We did, which was why lying about this was almost impossible. "Well, if I'm honest, I thought *you* were my mate."

She moved to the edge of the couch. "When? When did you think that?"

I waited a heartbeat, then dove right in with the truth bomb. "The moment I saw you standing across the bar that first night."

Her jaw dropped open. "Really?"

I nodded, partially annoyed that she hadn't realized when I had. Especially after the incredible night we'd shared.

"Yes, which was why I was totally blown away when I woke up the next day and found you were gone. During the night I thought you must have felt it too—the fated mate bond. But it's obvious you didn't then, and I guess it's equally as obvious, judging by the dumb-founded look on your face that you don't feel it now, either. So, I must have been wrong. If we were fated mates, both of us would have felt it."

Tears glimmered in Amy's eyes and I glanced away. I didn't want to see her shame at not feeling for me the way I felt for her. Worse, I couldn't bear to see her pity.

I stood up and walked away, pacing around the room and needing to move. "It's okay if you need to move back to town, Amy. I won't stop you from leaving if you don't want to be here."

Could she hear the pain in my tone? Finally, I turned to look at her. She was simply sitting there staring at me.

"We can organize some sort of custody thing, if you want. I can't walk away from Trixie now that I know she's alive. I already love her." I stopped, my chest tight and burning with pain.

Amy jumped to her feet. "I'd never take her from you. Never. I can see how much she means to you already. And... well, I can see how much *you* mean to *her*. She loves you too, Noah."

She does? It was something wonderful, at least, from this terrible situation.

If only Amy loved me, too.

I nodded and crossed my arms over my chest. "Thank you." Emotion clouded my voice, and I swallowed hard.

What else could I say? Amy had kept her from me for almost two years and I still believed she never would have brought her back to me if it wasn't for the wolf-like characteristics Trixie had begun to display.

"So that's it?" I asked, the tightness in my chest beginning to double up and burn. "You'll stay while we work out custody, then leave?"

She shook her head. "I need to tell you how I feel."

"You do?" I asked, my heart beating harder and faster in my chest. Did that mean there was more? That I could be... wrong?

She nodded. "Tammy pointed out to me that you didn't know how I felt about you, and this... relationship."

She gestured around us.

"No. I don't know how you feel," I said. "Everything you've said and done so far has revolved around the fact you were too ashamed to even wake up next to me, let alone tell me you were pregnant, or come to me for help with the baby."

She stared at me, more tears building in her eyes, turning them luminescent.

I pushed forward. "And I assume the only reason you're here is because Trixie has wolf genes, otherwise you'd still be in town, raising her on your own, and I would never have known I had a child at all."

Amy's tears overflowed then, slipping down her face, but she brushed them away. "You're right. I was a coward. I ran away from you, and I kept running."

"But why?" I demanded. "I would have cared for you, and loved you both! Was I really that scary that you had to leave and not come back for *two years*?"

Surely, I wasn't that ugly, or fearsome?

She shook her head. "It wasn't that. I wasn't afraid of you. I was afraid of myself. I'd convinced myself that I was weak, and naughty, and slutty for going home with you. I didn't want to be tempted again. So I stayed away."

"But what we have is fucking amazing! The attraction! The electricity in bed! That's what I've dreamt of my whole life. And I found it with you, Amy."

She shook her head. "Please don't say that."

"Say what? The truth?"

She put her hands over her ears like a child trying to block out a loud noise. "If that's the truth, then all that I've suffered and gone through—and all that I've kept from you in not allowing you to see our daughter till now—is for nothing and I'm not sure I can bear it. If I was wrong, then I've hurt us all, so badly..."

I stormed over to her and grabbed her hands, tugging them down so that she had no choice but to listen to me. "What are you talking about?"

"I convinced myself that you were... too sexy."

I huffed out a disbelieving laugh. "Thanks for the compliment, but not sure I'm understanding the problem yet."

"It *is* a problem! I don't feel like I have any control over myself with you! I feel weak... and stupid... and..."

I didn't let her finish the sentence. I grabbed her up in my arms and kissed her hard. I pressed my mouth into hers as though we were one person and not two. I separated her lips with mine so I could plunder her with my tongue.

When she moaned and grabbed for me, I picked her up and she wrapped her legs around my waist.

When she eventually broke our kiss, she panted out, "See, this isn't fair. It shouldn't hurt so much to be apart from you."

A groan ripped up through my chest as I carried her up the hallway and into our bedroom. I threw her onto the bed and tore at my clothes. She needed to feel how much I wanted her; know how much I needed her.

"This is how it's meant to be with a fated mate, Amy. You'll always need me. I'll always need you. And when we're apart, we'll yearn for one another like we're missing that other half of ourselves."

I threw my t-shirt on the ground and ripped off my jeans.

"That's what being a fated mate means."

Amy was lying on the bed, still clothed, tears in her eyes again. "Is that how it was for you too? Did you miss me over the two years I was gone?"

I stared at her, connecting our gazes. "Every damn day."

"Oh, God. So did I, Noah. I missed you so damn much."

I crawled onto the bed to make sure my mate knew just how much I had truly missed her.

CHAPTER 16

AMY

I grabbed for Noah's shoulders, desperate to feel his heavy body on mine. When I connected with his hot skin, I wrapped my fingers around his deltoids and pulled him down to kiss me again. We hadn't worked much out yet, but admitting finally that the feelings I had for him scared the shit out of me seemed to have unleashed something wholly amazing in him.

Was this just a bad case of lust? Or was this what being a fated mate felt like?

I knew in my heart this was not simply lust. I had never felt anything as strong as this pull toward Noah before, and I couldn't imagine ever feeling such a thing with anyone else.

I kissed him hard and moaned when he pulled back. "No. Don't go."

"Don't worry. I'm not going far," he said, putting only enough space between us to tug at my clothes.

I hurried out of my leggings and t-shirt with his help, then my underwear. I was hot and uncomfortable, and so ready to have his hands on me again. I wanted him. So much. And I didn't want to be afraid to want him anymore. If this was how it was meant to feel between us, why had I been so worried about it?

I pushed those thoughts to the back of my mind as he moved down my body.

I stopped him with a firm hand. "This time, it's my turn," I told him, pushing him back so that I could crawl on top of his huge, delicious body.

He lay back against the pillows with a lazy smile on his face. "Really? We get to take turns? Sounds pretty good to me."

I grinned back, excitement curling inside me. "Thank you."

"I'm all yours," he said, and even though there was a jesting tone in his voice, seriousness colored his blue eyes.

He was mine. All mine.

And he was letting me know it right here, and right now.

I kissed him gently on the mouth, then slid further down, exploring his body as he had mine. I kissed the indentation of his throat, and then his chest. Such beautiful thick muscles. It was hard not to gasp and moan at how hot he was.

I went lower, running my tongue around his abs and down one side of his hip into the sexy V that all women love on a really muscled guy. I couldn't believe such a man wanted to be in my bed.

When I reached his cock, already thick and hard, I took the flesh into my mouth and loved on him, sucking and licking his salty shaft until his gasps grew desperate and he tugged at my hair.

"Come up here," he said, his voice hoarse, like he'd been yelling.

After one more long lick, I crawled back up to him.

"Sit on my face," he demanded.

A blush swept up my cheeks. "I can't do that."

I was so wet and ready for him, and if I did that, there was no hiding from my desire. *How embarrassing.*

"Oh, yes, you can," he said, grabbing me around the waist and hauling me up his body.

I squealed at being manhandled, then grabbed onto the thick wooden headboard. My knees were on either side of his head and I was sitting on his chest staring down at his face. He shuffled down the mattress to get under me.

On that first lick of his tongue against my pussy, I screamed. I was so naked and exposed in this position. I wanted to hide, and yet I couldn't ask him to stop. It felt amazing to be pleasured like this, and my embarrassment floated away, to be replaced by nothing but need.

He grabbed my ass with both hands and ate my pussy like a starving man, flicking his tongue against my clit and tasting me as I cried out against the pleasure. Over and over again he licked me, nibbling at my throbbing flesh until I was so tight and ready, I was sobbing for release.

"Please. Don't stop. Please. I need more."

He pulled me down his body and held me over his cock.

"Ride me," he demanded, and I couldn't think of anything I'd rather do.

I settled on my knees, raised myself up, and slid back to find him. The head of his cock slipped between my folds—so wet already from my own desire, and from his mouth—and as I twisted my hips, his cock nudged inside of me.

I gasped at the feeling of pressure, wanting more. Needing him to assuage the ache inside of me. I dropped my head to kiss him, his hands on my waist tightening as I found his cock and pushed back to envelop him. I broke our kiss to gasp out my pleasure as he filled me. He gripped my hips and thrust up, meeting me halfway and making it impossible not to sob with how good the connection felt.

I began to move, riding his cock, up and down, getting faster and faster until my belly tightened to screaming point.

He took over then, grabbing my waist and pounding into me. I came, the sensation plowing through me in an unending wave of orgasmic, pulsating pleasure.

I dropped my head to his chest, and he groaned as he thrust deep inside me. Another orgasm hit just as he came inside me, my body greedily milking him as I shuddered on top of him. When I collapsed, I could barely breathe and had tears in my eyes.

I was finally whole. And happy.

"Oh God, I love you. I love you so much." I sobbed into his chest, finally feeling like I could tell him the truth about how I felt.

He wrapped his arms around me and squeezed me tight. Though he didn't say anything back, I knew he'd heard me. I didn't need any words back from him, in this moment. I felt his emotions in the beautiful, all-encompassing hug of his arms around me.

I sighed and closed my eyes, loving the sound of his heavy breathing in the room, and the feel of his thumping heart beneath our sweaty skin.

I rested with my head against Noah's shoulder. I was in the safest, best place in the world.

"I can't believe Trixie is still asleep," I said, grateful to my daughter for staying asleep long enough for this time to fix things between Noah and me.

"She's a good girl," he said, his voice more serious now than it had been earlier.

Eventually though, the atmosphere cooled, changed, and I knew it was time to slide off him and talk.

I rolled off him and sat up, wrapping myself partially in the sheet, since I knew this conversation was going to make me feel vulnerable enough. I didn't need to be naked for it, too.

He shuffled up the bed, grabbing the second pillow to put behind his head so he could rest comfortably against the headboard.

He nodded at me, all serious now. "You said you loved me."

I inhaled sharply. "Yes. Yes, I did."

I bit my lip and waited for him to continue.

He cocked an eyebrow at me. "Did you mean it?"

Surprise rippled through me. He still doubted? "Of course I meant it. I wouldn't say it if I didn't."

He glanced away. "I thought it might be just a, you know, heat of the moment thing."

I shook my head. "I think... I think I fell in love with you the moment I saw you too." Or at least I fell in lust. "But I didn't know anything about you then. Now... well, I've seen how respected you are in your community."

The Alpha had come to check on him in the first moments I'd arrived.

"And how you are with Trixie." My heart swelled at the thought of the two of them together. It took a special sort of man to bond so effortlessly with a little girl the way Noah had bonded with his daughter.

"So you did feel it," Noah said. "Even though you're not a wolf."

I nodded. "I felt something, very strong. Intense. Overwhelming. For you, that was probably a signal of the fated mate bond. But to me, it was terrifying. I'd never felt anything like it before, and it scared me half to death."

"Do you still feel that way?" he asked. "Terrified, I mean."

I shook my head. "I don't. Not now that I understand what it is. And that you might feel this crazy pull, too. If you feel the same way, then we're just two people in love. Nothing wrong with that. And nothing to be scared about, at all."

"Nothing at all," he said, reaching for my hand to link our fingers together. "So, you'll stay? Here? With me?"

Joy flooded through me. "I will if you'll have us."

Speaking of which.... I opened my mouth to tell him that our unprotected sex might have consequences, but Trixie called out to us.

I turned my head. "Trixie's awake."

"Let's go get her then," Noah said, swinging his legs over the side of the bed and getting to his feet, gloriously naked. In the past, I'd have averted my eyes, trying to avoid being so affected by his sexiness. Now, I drank my fill. I couldn't believe that this magnificent man loved me. And our daughter. It was like a dream coming true, and I so hoped I could make him as happy as I knew he would make me.

"Come on," he said when I hesitated, cocking his head to look back at me over his shoulder.

I laughed as I chased him down the hall, naked too. Who was here to see us and pass judgment? No one.

Noah pushed open the door and walked into the room, and I gloried in how happy he was to see his daughter. No one was going to love her the way he did. No one but me, of course. And that was exactly as it should be. Both of us here for her. And for each other.

"Mama," Trixie called, reaching out her arms for me.

I grinned at Noah as I walked around him to grab her.

"You do know that it's very possible I'm pregnant again," I said to Noah, hoisting our baby up out of her crib and holding her in my arms.

Noah blinked at me, stunned, before a wide grin split his face. "I hadn't even thought about it."

I laughed at him. "Seriously? Well, I suppose that's how we got into trouble the first time."

Noah grinned as Trixie reached for him. "Trouble? What are you talking about? This little one was meant to be."

He settled our daughter in his arms and dragged me into his side to join the hug. "We're a family, and I love you both. I'm not going anywhere, so if you are pregnant, then I'll be there, right by your side the whole time."

I sighed and closed my eyes, nestling into my big wolf shifter mate. "I can't think of anything I'd like more. Sounds like a dream come true, to me."

EPILOGUE

NOAH

Nine months later

I stared down at the pink, squealing little infant in my arms and my heart expanded in my chest. Love, as strong as what I felt for Amy and Trixie, flooded through me for my new son, and the woman who'd birthed him.

"He's absolutely perfect, Amy," I told her, as the midwife tied off the cord and helped to wrap him in a light blue, thin blanket.

"That's great." Amy panted, turning over to lie back on the bed after giving birth on all fours.

She looked happy but exhausted. To my eyes, she was still

perfect, but anxiety flared suddenly. "Is she okay?" I asked the doctor who was between Amy's legs and examining her still. Amy had been so concerned after her trauma around Trixie's birth, that we'd hired a specialist from the city to attend our home for the birth.

"She's very okay," the doctor said, and my anxiety died down to nothing. Thank God. Amy was my everything. Amy and our daughter. And now our perfect son.

"She did beautifully," the doctor added with a smile. "I'm just going to check for any tears, but there's no excessive bleeding, which is wonderful."

"Can I hold him?" Amy asked, putting her arms out for our son.

"Of course!" I walked him to her waiting and open arms.

She sighed as she took him, putting him straight to her breast. I kissed her forehead, which was hot and sweaty from exertion. "Do you want me to go and get Trixie? Or do you need some peace for a bit?"

Trixie was over two years old now and had started talking at a rate of knots. We couldn't get her to be quiet, even if we'd wanted to.

"Oh, I'd love to see her. Please," Amy said, stroking our newborn son's head. "I think she should meet her brother as soon as possible."

I nodded, thanked the doctor, and headed off to Kara's place to pick up Trixie. We were often at Ronan's house nowadays, their new little family enjoying the company of ours, and Trixie was besotted with the new Alpha heir.

As I walked up the street, I waved at my pack members and shot them thumbs up all round, and congratulations were shouted from every direction. I grinned, my chin high, and kept walking.

The past nine months hadn't been without their trials, but Amy and I had worked through them together, one obstacle at a time.

I'd learnt to trust her, letting go of the past and forgiving her the choices she had made surrounding Trixie's birth. I'd learnt that without that trust in one another, we couldn't build the relationship we both craved. So, I'd made the choice to accept what had been, and then to let it go and focus on the present and the future. And with that release had come the ability to truly love Amy, and be loved by her in return.

Neither of us were afraid of the fated mate pull any longer. Instead, we had come to cherish it as the gift it truly was.

Trixie seemed to be flourishing living here in the forest with the other children like her—one or two half-wolf, half-human children, and the rest full shifters. And Amy said she loved being part of such a tight-knit small community.

I was thrilled that everyone in the pack had accepted her and Trixie in without question. They were part of our pack now, and that would never change.

When I knocked on the door, Kara answered with her baby, Tennessee, on her hip. "Hey Noah! Is the baby here yet?"

"Yes! We have a beautiful and very healthy son. And Amy is doing very well, according to the doctor."

"That's wonderful! Congratulations," Kara said with a huge smile.

"Daddy!" Trixie cried, running toward me and hurling herself into my arms.

"Hey beautiful girl. Have you had a good day with Auntie Kara?"

"Oh, yes," she said with a smile, "but I wanna see Mama."

"Funny about that, because she wants to see you, too!" I hoisted Trixie higher in my arms and glanced back at Kara. "Thank you so much for keeping an eye on her for us."

"Of course! Anytime. Is Amy really doing okay?"

"She's doing beautifully," I said, pride blossoming in my chest. "Especially after everything she went through with Trixie's birth. You know how nervous I was when she wanted to try another natural birth, but it worked out perfectly, with the support in place. I'm so proud of her, though."

It had taken many chats with multiple doctors, and a lot of research, for Amy to want to try a natural birth this time around. I'd been happy to support whatever choice she wanted for her body either way, but I couldn't describe the level of pride I felt for her succeeding in her goal.

"She's an amazing woman, Noah. She is a perfect match for you."

"I know." I grinned happily at Kara, and gave Trixie, still in my arms, a little squeeze.

"Send my love, and I'll pop down later with dinner," Kara said. "It's just in the oven."

I grinned again at the Alpha's mate. "You're the best, Kara. Thanks."

Kara closed the door, and I took Trixie back home to see her mother.

"Guess what?" I said to her, as we went along the path.

"What Daddy?"

"Mama had the baby!"

Trixie screwed up her little face. "You mean the baby's here? Like... out of her tummy?"

"Yep. Out of her tummy. You have a little brother. Shall we go meet him?"

Trixie nodded, though I could see how concerned she was. We entered the house, still warm and heated for the birth.

"Mama, guess who's here?" I called out as I strolled up the hallway and into our bedroom.

Most of the mess had been cleaned away and new sheets already put on the bed. Amy still held the baby in her arms, against her naked body.

Trixie ran for the bed and jumped up beside her mother.

Amy put her arm around Trixie and whispered to her how much she loved her, and then told her all about her little brother. "He's too little now, but when he starts to grow, he's going to love his big sister Trixie so much."

"He will?"

"Of course, he will," Amy said. "He'll love you just as much as me and Daddy do."

Trixie peered at her brother, and then a smile graced her face.

"He's little," she said, and then reached over to touch his cheek with a gentle finger. "Nice."

Amy pressed a kiss to Trixie's forehead. "He is nice, and so are you, beautiful girl. I love you very much. So does Daddy."

I stood back and watched, reveling in the amazing woman my mate was. We'd overcome so much together.

Being by her side through the whole pregnancy had been a dream, and being at the birth was a miracle. I finally had the chance to experience everything I'd missed out on with Trixie, and now the circle of love was complete.

"Does Daddy wanna hold the baby so I can cuddle Trixie some more?" Amy asked me with a small wink.

I reached for our son. "Gladly."

My family.

Life was truly perfect.

THE END

CHAPTER 1

MANNIX

My father was a crazy, A-list asshole. I didn't like admitting it to anyone or saying the words out loud, but there was no changing the facts.

What sort of man, let alone an Alpha shifter, would drive his eldest child one hundred miles from home, leave him in the wilderness, and tell him to find his own way back?

Because that's exactly what my father did to my older brother, Reid, when he was eight years old.

For years, the pack believed Reid had died. What eight-year-old could survive the harsh winters of our state? After all, my father had chosen one of the most bitterly cold days of the year to drop Reid off. At least that was what I'd been told by others as I'd gotten older.

Within our pack, people would often gossip and speculate on how my brother had likely died. He'd been too young to shift. Too young to hunt. So how had my father ever expected him to survive? The simple truth was he probably hadn't. Which made my father... what? A murderer? Insane? Or both?

The pack said my father was cursed. And when he died in a fire a later that same year, no one had been surprised. He'd killed himself and my mother. I'd only been five years old at the time, so I don't remember much about that time.

I was saved by my father's best friend and the man who raised me, Alfred. A kind man. A loving beta who took on the role of Alpha after my father's passing, only because there was no one else in the pack to do it.

But the biggest shock of all had come the night before Alfred died. He confided in me that he'd heard whispers that my brother Reid was still alive.

I hadn't wasted any time. In the same week that I buried the man who'd raised me, I set off in the same direction my father had apparently driven off in with my brother all those years ago. I'd traveled from pack to pack, asking everyone I met about a man named Reid.

Eventually, I found someone who knew of a man with an Alpha's size, height and strength. He was apparently quiet but a good leader. That description sounded just like the man I'd always envisioned my brother would have been. But was it him? And what would the passage of time have done to him?

I turned off the engine of my truck and stared out the front window at the buildings set around this village square. I'd been driving for a month, and I finally arrived at the Northwood pack grounds.

My heart pounded a little too hard in my chest and after all this time, I hesitated to get out of the vehicle.

Suddenly a fist pounded on my window, and I jumped, glaring at the guy staring at me.

"Can I help you?" he called out.

I sighed and pulled the keys out of the ignition before pushing open the door, my hesitation at an end.

"Hey, man." I shut the door and slid the keys into my jeans pocket.

"Hey," he repeated. "Are you looking for someone?"

My heart thudded again, sending stress bucketing through my system. "Yeah. I'm looking for Reid."

The guy's eyebrows fluttered high on his forehead and his eagle-like gaze scraped over me. "Oh, yeah? I was heading over there myself to have a chat with the Alpha. Wanna tag along?"

I inhaled sharply, a pain like being kicked in the gut hitting me square in the solar plexus. "Sure. I'm Mannix, by the way."

I held out my hand and the other guy took it, shaking my whole arm with the strength of his grip. "I'm Jason. Come on. They should be home now."

"They?" I asked, walking side by side with the guy who had to be one of the pack's betas. He was large and looked fit but was still an inch or two shorter than me.

"Yeah, the Alpha and her family."

"*Her* family?" I repeated. "Your Alpha is a... her?" How did that work? Didn't Jason say we were going to see Reid?

Jason frowned at me. "I thought you said you knew Reid."

"I do... kind of," I muttered as we stepped up in front of a large log house. It was double story and surrounded by gardens.

I glanced around. It was the only two-story house in the area. "This is the Alpha's house," I said, knowing I was correct without needing Jason to confirm it.

Jason frowned at me, suspicious now of a stranger, which made him a good beta. "I think you're going to have to explain to me what you're doing here before I let you in to see Allara and Reid."

"Allara?" I repeated. "Is that my brother's mate?"

"Brother?" Jason gasped, his shock visible in the way his frown disappeared, and his mouth dropped open.

I wanted to smack myself in the head. "Look. I..." I'd royally fucked this up. I hadn't wanted it to come out like that. "My brother went missing twenty years ago. His name was Reid. We all thought he'd died, but I was told only a week ago that he was still alive."

"So, you're here to find out if our Reid is your brother?" Jason asked. A grin stretched across his mouth.

"Yeah. Sort of." I glanced at the house, then back to Jason. "What's this Reid like?"

Jason assessed me, crossing his arms over his chest and staring me down. I must have passed some kind of test because he relaxed a notch. "You kinda look like him, you know."

"I do?"

Jason nodded. "Yeah. Same eyes, and that cleft in your chin. Anyway, Reid's a great guy. He's mated to our Alpha, Allara."

"Was he born in the pack?" I asked, hoping he wasn't and assuming that Jason wouldn't waste my time if he was.

Jason shook his head. "No. He was a foundling. One of our women discovered him in the forest, half dead, starving and dehydrated, when he was about ten."

Ten? Jesus. He'd survived two *years* out there, on his own?

"Or that's what we all thought because he was tall. They never found out where he came from, and he wouldn't talk about it. Was mute for months after they found him, but he came good."

Every word was like a punch to my heart. "They... you..." I swallowed hard, tears clogging my throat. "You found him?"

"Not me." Jason said, shaking his head. "Emma. She raised him."

I stared at the large house, too many emotions to mention running through my mind. "What's he like now?"

"Why don't you come meet him yourself?" Jason said, knocking me in the shoulder as he walked past me and headed up toward the entrance. "Come on."

I was rooted to the spot. How did I approach the man who

should be my Alpha? The man my father had thrown away as if he were trash.

"I..."

Jason groaned, turned away and knocked on the door.

Oh, fuck.

The door opened and a woman answered, a baby in her arms.

My stomach clenched tight in my abdomen, adrenaline coursing along my veins. I wanted to run. Away, preferably. And yet I couldn't move at all. Indecision froze me.

Jason spoke to the woman. I had to assume she was the aforementioned Allara, then they both started to walk toward me.

My feet shifted on the spot where I stood, and I was glad to learn that I could still move.

"Hi, there," the woman said as she moved closer. The babe in her arms only looked a few weeks old but was content and sleeping. "I'm Allara, the Alpha of the Northwood Pack. Jason says you're looking for Reid."

I nodded, swallowing hard. "I'm Mannix."

She smiled softly. "And you're looking for Reid?" she repeated.

"Did Jason tell you?"

Allara glanced at her beta. "He did. He said you might be part of Reid's family. He never talked about the time before my pack found him, so I don't really know what to say or do."

"My father was our pack's Alpha," I said swiftly, wanting to get the information out as quickly as possible. "Your husband is my older brother, if your Reid is the same Reid I'm looking for."

I sounded like a bumbling idiot, but I didn't really care. Well, I did, but my pride was a small price to pay if I got my brother back.

Allara smiled broadly this time. "I think it's safe to say that he is. How many other men are the size of an Alpha, but were found wandering the woods alone when they were a child?"

Jason frowned at me suddenly. "Was your father sick?"

"Sick?" I tilted my head, pretending to think about it. Mentally sick? Probably. But how could I explain that in this moment? I ignored the question for now. "My parents died in a fire."

"Oh my God." Allara's hand covered her mouth. "I'm so sorry."

"It's okay." I shrugged off her concern. "It was a long time ago."

An entire lifetime ago, for me. I barely remembered my parents, and from what I'd been told about my father, I was glad I didn't recall much.

"Okay, well, Reid should be back any minute. He went out for dinner a little while ago. He won't be long."

Allara's gaze slid past me, and her face lit up like it was Christmas morning. "There he is. Reid!"

She waved her free arm in the air like she was hailing a cab.

I turned slowly and stared as a huge man walked toward us. They'd said he was Alpha-sized, but this man was even bigger than I'd expected.

His eyes were dark as was his hair, and in his chin, I saw the family cleft that neither of us had escaped.

This man was my brother. I was certain of it.

He walked up and went straight to his mate's side, possessively sliding a hand around her waist while simultaneously dropping a kiss on top of her head.

Only then did he turn his attention to me. "Hey, I'm Reid." He introduced himself with an easy smile, not a glimmer of recognition on his face.

"Hey." I nodded at the large man, no doubt staring like a wide-eyed fool.

Allara frowned at me, then glanced up at Reid. "Sweetheart, this is Mannix."

I wasn't sure if it was my name or if he suddenly recognized something in my features, but Reid's face transformed. His eyebrows drew together, and his mouth dropped open.

"Man... Did you say, Mannix?"

He was staring at me now with suspicion etched into every line in his face.

I nodded. "Yeah. That's me."

"Jason, take Allara and the baby into the house for me," Reid said, and his tone brooked no argument.

He was all Alpha, from the commanding voice to the straightening of his spine, to the flaring of his nostrils.

He didn't even look at his mate or Jason, he simply directed Allara into Jason's arms and stepped in front of them.

Allara threw me a worried look before she did as Reid had asked and walked back into the house.

The aggression in his stance was sparking the Alpha also in my bloodline. I pushed down my wolf as he rose inside my chest. He wanted to protect me from the threat Reid posed. I'd been raised by Alfred to be the Alpha of my pack, and every part of me wanted to respond to the anger Reid was throwing my way.

But I would not fight him, no matter what happened. I forced my wolf to calm through sheer willpower.

Reid crossed his arms over his chest and stared me down as if sensing the struggle inside me. "What the fuck are you doing here, Mannix? What do you want?"

www.ingramcontent.com/pod-product-compliance
Lightning Source LLC
Chambersburg PA
CBHW071013180726
48291CB00004B/1444